About the author

James Fitzsimmons was born in Whiston, Lancashire. He studied Social Sciences (Economics) at Liverpool Polytechnic, and Media at Cumbria College of Art and Design. He has had work broadcast, poetry published and created successful concepts for animation and books. He has enjoyed living in Cumbria for the last 21 years.

Book One

Journey to Mailcann

Journey to Mailcann

James Fitzsimmons

Clyke Books

First published in Great Britain in 2007 by
Clyke Books
17 Cherry Tree Crescent
Kendal
Cumbria
LA9 5EN
www. clykes.co.uk

ISBN 978-0-9556442-0-7

A CIP record for this book is available
from the British Library

Printed by Lintons Printers, County Durham
on recycled paper

for Suzanne

For thousands of years, Clykes had made their homes in abandoned badger setts and among tree roots deep in the wild woods. Many centuries ago, human beings, known to the Clykes as Talluns, divided up the land. They felled woodlands and built hundreds of miles of dry-stone walls around their pastures. And so the traditional Clyke homelands were destroyed. All was not lost, however, for during this period of intense wall building, the Clykes took advantage of the prospect that had presented itself for them to acquire new homes.

When the Tallun wall builders finished work for the day, the Clykes would clear out the space beneath the lower throughstones in the newly built wall by removing the small filler stones, or heartings. These they placed back onto the stone heaps, concealing their interior handiwork with strategically placed rocks. Coming to work next day, the Talluns would not notice anything amiss. When the stretch of wall was completed, the Clykes left their temporary accommodation in hayricks and rabbit holes and settled in the walls. The chambers under the throughstones were transformed into snug dwellings in which the Clykes thrived.

Clykes only ever live on farms where traditional, true methods of farming exist; some call these farms organic. Clykes keep the farms in good heart. They soothe and reassure the stock, stave off many dangers, prevent disease and forewarn of threats. They nurture the crops, use and replenish wild plants and have a great store of herbal knowledge. The farms they inhabit are fertile and bounteous. A prosperous Tallun and well-kept farm guarantees plenty for all.

Sometimes a Tallun going about his work will catch a glimpse of a Clyke out of the corner of his eye: a tiny, scurrying brown thing vanishes into the bracken: a small, unrecognisable creature rushes out of the grass to disappear into a hole in a wall. Mistaking them for some small animal and thinking no more about it, the Tallun goes on his way.

Chapter One

Within the oak woods of Cappledale, a deserted mill stood beside a broad, deep pool. The old stone building had fallen into decay, its waterwheel gone, long rotted away. All that could be seen of the mill race that once fed the wheel with water was the vague outline of its course in the grass where a line of tall alders now grew.

At the edge of a clearing near to the mill, Sabrax and Dorcan Clyke were busy working. Sabrax, who stood no taller than a starling, was dressed in dark brown clothes and chestnut coloured boots. He had green eyes and dark eyebrows. Like other Clykes, Sabrax wore his black hair long. The two Clykes had already filled several hessian sacks with twigs and carried them into their wall. Sabrax brushed up the remaining twig litter into a small pile.

'We've done well,' said Dorcan.

Sabrax nodded, sweeping the pile onto Dorcan's shovel. Dorcan was a little plumper than his brother, with dark brown hair and had twinkling black eyes like those of a mouse. He, too, was dressed all in brown. He raised his shovel up and slid the twig litter carefully into his sack.

'That's it,' said Sabrax, 'that'll do for today.'

'You sure?'

'Sure.'

Dorcan swung the bag of twigs over his shoulder as Sabrax gathered up the shovels and brushes. The two Clykes walked quickly back towards their home in the wall.

Slipping silently from a high ledge on the river cliffs, Krokr Longtoe, the hawk, glided across the dale on outstretched wings. As he flew, he kept his eyes fixed firmly on the two Clykes walking beside the dry-stone wall. Folding his wings slightly to increase his speed, Krokr banked sharply and set his line of attack.

Sabrax reached the front door first. Pushing it open, he went in, unaware that his brother had tripped over a plant root, lost his balance and was being driven forward uncontrollably by the weight of his load. Nor was he aware of Krokr Longtoe swooping, striking out and missing the stumbling Clyke. Sabrax turned round in the hallway as Dorcan crashed onto the hall floor, spilling his bag of twigs.

'I'm sorry.'

'Anyone can trip over,' said Sabrax, looking down at his brother, 'you needn't look so upset.'

'What on earth was it?' Dorcan's face was ashen.

Sabrax slammed the stout front door shut and slid the large iron bolt into place.

'A plant root, I expect,' he said, helping Dorcan up.

'I don't mean that. As we came in - something struck me on the shoulder.'

Sabrax unlocked the door. The brothers dashed back outside and looked around. Over to the west, the blood red sun was sinking behind a far hillside. The only sounds in the winter afternoon were those made by a flock of chacking jackdaws flying to their roost and the water from the mill pool tumbling over the weir.

'Well, whatever it was, it's not there now,' said Sabrax, 'come on, we're going to miss supper.'

'Supper? Oh, yes. What is for supper?'

'Cheese and pignut pie. Our favourite. But it'll be leftovers if we don't get those twigs bagged up fast.'

Dorcan and Sabrax went back inside, closing the door.

*

The widow Calamorica Clyke presided over her immediate family of two sons, Sabrax and Dorcan, two daughters, Rosmanda and Woadica, her own brothers, Durabito and Longalio, and over the wider tribe of Cappledale Clykes. She and her family all sat in high backed chairs around the dining table. They had finished eating supper. Large pottery dishes and plates, which earlier had been stacked with dried nettle fritters, fern head casserole, parsnip surprise, cheese and pignut pie, beech mast bakes, and big willow baskets that had been filled with borage buns, now lay in disarray on the table. All were empty.

'That was a lovely meal,' declared Calamorica, mopping up the last of the juice on her plate with a slice of bread, 'lovely.'

She pushed her plate away. Calamorica's face was handsome but ruddy from her open-air life. She had silver grey hair and wore a smart brown bonnet on her head. Pinned to the bonnet was a red jewel set in a gold mount that held a long feather in place. A carved wooden box lined with crimson velvet lay open on the table near to Calamorica's right hand.

'Who's going to tell us a story?' asked Calamorica.

She raised her large earthenware goblet and swallowed a mouthful of mallow brose. She glanced at the other Clykes seated around the table. 'Mm? Who's it to be?'

The Clykes there gazed vacantly at the walls or sank lower in their chairs.

'What about you, Durabito? You haven't told one for ages.'

Durabito had blue eyes and a head of hair as white as a newly washed sheep fleece. He stared at his sister, knowing full well she was about to take advantage of him.

'I told you a story only last week.'

'Well, we want another one, don't we everybody?' said Calamorica petulantly, flouncing back in her chair. 'What are you waiting for?'

'Oh, er, nothing. Right.'

Durabito stood up from his seat. He cleared his throat, rested his hands on the table, smiled at everyone and began his story.

'A, er, a long time ago . . . '

'How long?' queried Calamorica, sweeping a breadcrumb from her chest.

'It was early summer in the year of the Great Winter,' he recounted, gazing intently at Calamorica, who wriggled in her chair.

'What are you looking at me for?'

Durabito arched his eyebrows, glanced up at the ceiling and muttered under his breath. He addressed the others seated around the table.

'And the dale was alive with Talluns and horses going about their daily work. Some of the Talluns were busy in their workshops making waggons and wheels, while others turned trees into tables, chairs and beds. At this time of year the Talluns clipped the flocks of sheep with big metal shears. It was a great occasion. Wooden barrels of beer were set up and large trays of food brought out from the farmhouse. There was plenty of everything for those Clykes to share . . . '

'How lovely,' exclaimed Calamorica, 'plenty for everyone.'

'A dance was to be held,' continued Durabito, 'to celebrate the end of the shearing. A certain Tallun who played the fiddle was to provide the music for the celebrations, but he had fallen ill. The Talluns of the village had plied him with all manner of things to try and cure him. None of them had worked . . . '

'Not surprised,' muttered Calamorica.

'Our ancestors saw what was happening and decided that they would provide a remedy for his illness . . . '

'That's more like it,' cried Calamorica, 'carry on.'

'In order to dispense the potion, they had to enter the fiddler's house. That night, when everyone was asleep, a Clyke . . . '

'Which one?'

Durabito gave Calamorica a long hard look.

'Er, Snod the Wise,' he said, quickly making up the

name.

'Snod,' said Calamorica, 'ye-sss. I've heard of him.'

'Crept into the house through a hole in the wall and made his way up a ladder to the fiddler's bedroom. The fiddler was feverish. Snod climbed up onto his bed. He stood in front of the fiddler's face and poured the potion into his mouth. The fiddler opened his eyes, stared at Snod standing there on his chest, and fainted away. In the morning the fiddler awoke. He was as fit as a cow fed on cauliflower. The rest of the Talluns were amazed at his recovery and that night the fiddler played at the dance. Everyone there said he was the best fiddler in all the Dales.'

Durabito sat down. The rest of the Clykes at the table applauded his story. He looked at Calamorica. She was smiling and dabbing her eyes with a handkerchief.

'That was wonderful. What a lovely story, Durabito. Thank you.'

After supper, Rosmanda, a fine looking Clyke with large hazel eyes and long red hair, joined Calamorica, Sabrax and Uncle Durabito. They remained at the table in Long Hall, seated at the end nearest the fire. An old games board had been set out on the table and six playing pieces, carved to represent different trees, stood before each of the players. Some of the playing pieces were cracked, others were damaged or chipped and their once-bright colours had faded.

Rosmanda rattled the die in a horn cup and tipped it out on the table.

'One. Pass.'

'It'll snow soon,' said Calamorica, attempting to break their concentration.

Sabrax and company showed no interest in her observation. Durabito swept up the die in the horn cup, rattled it vigorously and spilled it on the table.

'Four. Lovely little four. Oak.'

Durabito slid his piece onto the board with a flourish.

Calamorica got up from her seat, went across to the hearth, took a log from the basket and pushed it onto the back of the fire. A great shower of sparks flew up the chimney. The players stared at her.

'Are you trying to put us off?' asked Sabrax tetchily.

'Me? No.'

Calamorica sat down again. The log on the fire began to hiss. Sap bubbled out. Ignoring the new distraction, Sabrax, Rosmanda and Durabito again studied the pieces already out on the board. With a great roar the log on the fire burst into flames, the light from it casting great Clyke shadows onto the Hall walls. Slowly the players turned and stared at Calamorica.

'Did you manage to get in all of the twigs, Sabrax?'

'Shhhhhhhhhhhhhh,' he hissed.

Sabrax rattled the die in the horn cup and tipped it out on the table.

'Five. Not bad. Not bad at all. Elm, I think.' He pushed his piece out onto the board.

'What's that?' asked Calamorica.

'What's what?' replied Durabito warily, suspecting it was a ploy on his sister's part, to distract him.

'That,' said Sabrax, getting suddenly to his feet.

Now the Clykes all listened intently. A distant rumble rose up. Soon it had turned to strong vibrations that coursed through the ground beneath their feet. It rattled their chairs, the table and the pieces on the board. Their furled battle flag slid to the floor. Two suits of armour standing beside the doorway clanked, pieces on the board fell over and the beans in the bowl jumped about as the vibrations grew into tremors that shook the very stones in the wall. Longalio dashed into Long Hall.

'Quick, everyone, to the ladders.'

The Clykes hurriedly scaled the ladders that linked each level within the wall. They emerged among the camstones on the top and watched as a huge red lorry made its way, little by little, up the narrow winding lane towards them. Suddenly the lorry's headlights swept across the wall. The Clykes drew back among the stones. As the lorry passed by, diesel fumes billowing from its exhaust blew over the Clykes, leaving them coughing and spluttering in its wake. A shiny silver pick-up followed the lorry up the lane. The driver glowered and stared straight ahead. Standing up in the back of the pick-up was a large dog. The creature spotted the Clykes among the stones. It growled and bared its teeth.

'Must be the new Tallun,' speculated Longalio.

'Our new neighbour. Not the cheeriest of Talluns, I'd say,' stated Calamorica, as the pick-up's brakes squealed.

'I don't like the look of him,' said Dorcan.

'We'd better go and see what he's about, first thing in the morning.'

'I'm sure we'll be able to manage him, Mother,' said Sabrax.

'I've no doubt about that.'

*

Next morning, after breakfast, the Clykes set out for the

new Tallun's farm. Sabrax led the way. He walked on ahead briskly, a sense of purpose about him. When they reached the farm gate, the Clykes saw the huge red lorry rolling down the farm drive towards the cattle grid. They took refuge in a wall. In daylight, the Tallun word "Removals" clearly showed on the side of the lorry and from their place of safety, the Clykes watched as it rattled over the grid and drove away down the lane. They crept out from among the stones.

'Come on,' urged Sabrax, 'let's go.'

The Clykes plunged into the grasses and hurried towards the farmhouse. Several minutes later, they reappeared at the edge of the yard.

'What a lot of strange stuff he's got,' said Dorcan.

A tall stack of spindly wooden chairs stood outside on the cobbles by the front door to the farmhouse, along with several carpets, a dozen tea chests, assorted boxes of different sizes, a bird cage on a stand, piles of books, two beds, two mattresses, a collection of pictures in ornate frames, several curtain poles, an old vacuum cleaner, an even older garden mower, assorted spades, rakes and other garden tools. The new Tallun was busy carrying his possessions into his new home.

'Follow me,' said Sabrax.

He set off across the yard. The others went after him, stooping under an iron gate in a wall and gaining the side of the house without being seen. The Clykes formed a pyramid against the wall under the front room window. Sabrax scrambled to the top.

'Well,' shouted Calamorica, 'what can you see?'

'Nothing much,' he said, peering in, 'just loads of boxes.'

The farm dog's head slammed against the window pane.

'Oaahoh,' shouted Sabrax, losing his balance.

The dog drew its head away and attacked the window again, white teeth bared, barking in a frenzy.

Sabrax fell backwards and slid down over the rest. The pyramid collapsed into a jumble of bodies, Clykes panicking and thrashing about as they tried to untangle themselves. The dog still barked and gradually obscured the lower window panes with stains impressed by its wet nose. Clykes got to their feet and ran. Sabrax was last up. He scuttled into the garden shrubbery as the Tallun came to the window.

The Tallun looked out. On the overgrown square of lawn a rabbit sat hunched.

'Only a blasted rabbit,' shouted the Tallun, 'you've seen a rabbit before. What's the matter with you?'

The dog slunk away. It hid behind a box in a corner of the room.

*

Chapter Two

A giant pine tree stood in the middle of a forest. On the uppermost branch, Krokr Longtoe was asleep, perched on one leg, his other leg drawn tight into his body feathers. His head was folded in under his wing. In his dreams he hunted down Clykes, flying through the air after them as they fled in terror. Oh, how easy it was to swoop and take a Clyke in his talons. He spared none and did not stop until he'd cleared the dale of their presence. Now he alone ruled, flying high, with the sun on his back, stooping and taking a bird or small animal whenever he pleased. Krokr Longtoe, lord of the fields and forests. Then into his dream, as in many other nights before, came a loud hiss. Krokr was jolted awake. He gazed wide-eyed at the trees in the silent forest and panted. His heart beat loudly in his breast. Realising he had woken from a dream, he blinked and settled again, sliding his head back under his wing.

*

Late one evening, before the hay harvest, Sabrax sat alone in an armchair in front of the fire, studying his woodcarving of a hen pheasant and her seven chicks. All was peaceful now in Long Hall, though earlier on there had been a clamour of voices as the plans for the autumn had been discussed among the Clykes. There had always been evenings like these, of course, during the preceding two thousand years, where a great hum of anticipation and excitement accompanied the belief that this year would be the best ever. Now the rest of the Clykes were asleep in their beds, dreaming of crops so heavy that even the great flocks of birds couldn't finish the surplus. Sabrax yawned loudly. He got up out of his chair and put his carving down on the sideboard top.

Calamorica had hung her bonnet on the back of a chair, the red jewel in its golden mount holding the long feather in place. Sabrax gathered the bonnet up.

'The talisman,' he muttered, 'the most precious of our possessions - left lying around.'

He unpinned the brooch; the feather slid out and fell onto the table. For a moment he held the brooch in the palm of his hand, studying the intricate metalwork, wondering what its origins were. Who had made it all those centuries ago? He put the brooch back in its carved wooden box, snapped the lid shut and carried it across to the fireplace. One of the stones in the chimney breast had been fixed on a pivot; he pushed it with his finger and it swung back, revealing a secret void. He placed the box in the void and closed the stone over again.

A black iron cauldron filled with water stood on the hearth. Sabrax picked it up by its handle and set it on the glowing embers. Apart from the steady tick of the clock, the only other sound in the room was the slow whine of the water as it began to warm up. He got his coat from the back of a chair, pulled on his boots and made his way silently to the front door. Opening it, Sabrax slipped out for a last look at the evening.

In the distance a dog barked. The wind had lessened, but still it shook and rustled the grasses beside the path as Sabrax ambled along. He came to the small beck that ran through their farm, pausing for a moment in the middle of the plank bridge to listen to it bubbling over the stones. He thought the noisy water sounded like so many voices. Above, the sky was clear. Sabrax gazed up at the mass of stars and sighed. He was fascinated by the stars, but never quite understood why they turned in the sky. Or from where the moon appeared. Or where it went to when it set. Or why it shrank to a thin crescent and vanished, only to grow again. It was all very perplexing.

He had become chilled in the cool night air. A shiver ran through him. He set off briskly along the path beside the beck and followed it until it ran into a shallow mere. He visited the mere most days, liking it in all its moods and in all weathers. In winter the water froze and Clykes ventured out from the comfort of their wall to skate on the ice. In spring frogs spawned in the clear water and the fry of fish darted and swam about in shoals. Now, in summer, it was home to coot and moorhen, whose tiny young raced over the water. Sometimes mallard came there and One Eye the heron, so named since Calamorica blinded one eye with her knife when he had seized her in his bill and tried to eat her. A raft that Sabrax and Dorcan had built from ash branches lay hidden in the reeds below the bank. The brothers liked to sail the raft across to the island in the middle of the mere. Sabrax stood for a moment looking at the water, then walked on.

A sudden movement on the path ahead stopped him in his tracks. He stared and listened hard. There was something out there. It whirred, panted, flapped, creaked and squeaked. In the blackness he could see two large yellow discs that appeared to hover in the air. Sabrax crept forward. He raised his hand until it rested on the flap of his mustard pouch. His mouth was as dry as oat husks. He couldn't swallow, his legs trembled and his feet felt as heavy as stones. Moving in closer, he saw at last that the yellow disks were two large eyes - owl eyes. They blinked at him as he hesitated on the path. But this wasn't a giant tawny owl that swooped silently out of the wood at night to catch a careless Clyke. It was one of the little owls that lived about the walls and ate beetles and moths. Oblivious to all threats now in his concern for the creature, Sabrax strode forward.

'Great badger beards, Owl, what's happened to you?'

'A Clyke, you're a Clyke. Oh thank goodness for that. I'm trapped.' The bird pointed to its feet with the tip of a wing. 'It hurts - the pain. I'm certain I heard a nasty weasel in the grass.'

Going into the surrounding grasses, Sabrax thrashed about in it long enough to make sure no weasel lurked there. He walked back to the owl.

'Look at your legs, bound in loops of cast-off nylon fishing line.'

Sabrax knelt down beside the bird. The line had cut

deep into the bird's flesh. The owl stood in a small pool of dark red blood.

'I don't know how I managed to get so tangled up. I landed on the ground over there and before I knew it, I'd walked right into the middle of this lot.'

'You stay still and keep quiet, Owl. I'll be back as fast as I can.'

Sabrax stood up and straight away ran off along the path towards home.

'Please come back, please,' whimpered the owl after him.

When he reached home, Sabrax ran into Long Hall, to the small cupboard set into the wall beside the hearth. He opened the door, quickly taking out a bandage and two small jars. He hurried back to the hallway, stuffing the items into his coat pocket. His knife and belt hung on a peg by the front door. He grabbed them as he passed, fastened the belt around his waist and pulled the brass buckle tight. He closed the front door and raced away.

The owl watched Sabrax warily as he climbed in among the tangle of twigs and nylon line.

'This stuff's left by lazy fisher Talluns. They don't care what damage it causes. Creatures snared in it are doomed - er, without help, I mean.'

Sabrax drew his knife from its sheath and concentrated on his task. He worked urgently. The blade's keen edge made short work of the nylon strands and soon he was down to the last loop of line. He cut it. It parted with a ping.

'That's the last strand, Owl. You're free.'

'Ohhh, what sweet relief. I can feel the blood surging back.'

The owl opened and closed his toes. Sabrax stood to one side and watched the owl limping painfully up and down in front of him.

'If you hadn't come along, I would have been gone from this world by morning. No more flying around the walls for me. I would have been an easy meal for a stoat, or a mink, or a . . . '

'Fox?' Sabrax suggested mischievously.

'Oh, don't, don't. I can't bear to think about it.'

The owl closed his eyes in horror at Sabrax's suggestion. Sabrax knelt down. He took out the bandage and jars from his coat pocket and began to bind the owl's legs.

'You've saved my life,' said the owl, sighing deeply. 'How can I ever repay you?'

'You could keep watch for us, be an extra pair of eyes.'

'I could, couldn't I. Yeee-sss, keep watch over you. I'm up on the wall tops and in the trees all the time. I could do that with my feet tied. Here, d'you get it? Do it with my feet tied.' He laughed, roused his feathers and shook his wings vigorously.

'All done.' Sabrax stood up and looked at his neat dressings. 'That's woundwort I've put on - it'll heal your cuts in no time at all.'

'What's your name?'

'Sabrax, Sabrax Clyke.'

'Thank you, Sabrax. Now I must be off. I've three owlets to feed. They'll be wondering where I've got to.'

Sabrax stood back. The owl flew up into the air and

circled about.

'Thank you again,' it shrieked. 'I'll look out for you all, never fear.'

It went off on silent wings into the night.

*

'You must be hungry after your journey, Pymbo,' said Cataporinganio, 'it's a long way from Cappledale to here.'

The old wizard settled back in his armchair. He crooked his finger and stroked the head of the ring ouzel perched on his right hand.

'Can I offer you something to eat?'

'What do you have?' replied Pymbo, looking quizzically at him.

'Whatever takes your fancy. Anything.'

'Anything?'

'In the whole wide world,' said the wizard, smiling and nodding his head.

Pymbo roused up his feathers with a vigorous shake of his body. Then the feathers, each one shining with a healthy bloom, settled slowly back until they formed again Pymbo's sleek outline.

'In that case, I'd like something - special.'

'Oh?'

'Brandling worms. Fresh from a compost heap, please.'

'Brandling worms it is.'

The room in which Cataporinganio and Pymbo sat was one of seven the wizard had hewn out of the granite mountain. A huge, bare, oak shield hung on the wide chimney breast above the white limestone mantelpiece. Black peat smouldered in the fire grate and scented the room. Polished rectangles of blue slate slab, randomly laid, formed the floor and were covered by a large, remarkably patterned and brightly coloured, woollen carpet. Four tall oak chairs, their arm rests carved with dragon heads, stood in a line beside an ornately carved desk on which dusty scrolls, papers, quill pens, a knife, a sand shaker, pots of ink, a stuffed vole and strands of dried seaweed were scattered. On either side of the single window, hundreds of old leather-bound books had been stacked against the wall. Fixed on a tripod and set at an angle, a long brass telescope pointed out through the window at the night sky. A glass case containing dozens of coloured bottles stood on the windowsill, each one was full of liquid and clearly labelled.

Cataporinganio stared hard at the beaten copper bowl standing on a carved oak table next to his armchair. He whispered incantations under his breath. He raised his hand. A large gemstone set in a gold ring on his middle finger began to glow.

'Won't be a second, Pymbo. It's warming up. Haven't used it in ages.'

A streak of white light arced between gemstone and bowl. Pymbo was blinded momentarily, but when his eyes focused again, he saw that the bowl was filled with wriggling brandlings.

'Will that be enough?'

'Plenty. What about you?'

'I'm not hungry. I had a meal ten nights ago. Now then, what is it that brings you here to my mountain?'

Pymbo sucked in a brandling with his beak and swallowed it.

'Mmm. Lovely. Very tasty. I am come from Durabito

Clyke, Cataporinganio, to invite you as guest of honour to the two hundredth birthnight of his sister, Calamorica. It is to be celebrated at their home.'

'Then you must tell him I accept.'

*

Sabrax, a mug of dandelion tea in his hand, stood for a moment in front of the door to Woadica's workshop. He knocked twice and went in.

'Hello, Sabs. You all right?'

'Mmm. Brought you some tea, fresh from the pot.'

'That is kind of you.'

Woadica took the mug from him. She had a sip. She cleared a space on her workbench and put the mug down on a square of scrap canvas. Woadica had a delicate face, large brown eyes and hair the colour of barley.

'Just what I need.'

Lying on the workbench were two pairs of new green boots. Sabrax picked up a pair.

'Who are they for?'

'One pair's for mother for her birthnight and the other's for the message Clyke to take to Borengapor.'

'Ah, Borengapor. Yes. How's Bannanua? Has Borengapor mentioned her lately?'

'No.'

'Oh.'

'Why? Is there anything the matter?'

'No. No. No. Just wondering, that's all. I'll, er, leave you to it, then.'

He put the boots back down on the workbench, nodded and ambled out. He was closing the workshop door when Woadica called after him.

'Oh, Sabrax.'

The door opened and he reappeared.

'Bannanua's fine, as a matter of fact.'

He grinned, closed the door and went away whistling.

*

The wind stirred the green leaves on a tall ash, dappled sunlight splashing Krokr Longtoe's plumage. Sabrax emerged from the wall, unaware of being watched by a pair of eyes so sharp they could see striations on a pin at a hundred paces. He glanced around warily. Up in the tree Krokr's feet and talons tightened on the branch, as he made ready to swoop. Sabrax, ever cautious, ran straight out from the wall to disappear under the overhanging shelter of a clump of brambles. Krokr relaxed, drew his foot back into his feathers and waited again.

*

Chapter Three

Of all the Clykes, Longalio was the most skilled. He worked in wood and metal and got his raw materials from the farm tip. After night had fallen, he would go and search through the rubbish that had been dumped over the years in a deep hollow in the wood. If he found a discarded, bent table fork, he would turn it into four handy knives in his workshop, cutting off the tines, then hammering them flat on his anvil and sharpening their edges. An old, unwanted bread tin made an excellent bath. All of the bowls, pans, bedsteads, cupboards, doors, chests and wardrobes in the Clykes' dwelling within the wall had been made from scrap metal and wood.

It was late evening. Longalio was in his workshop. His latest piece of handiwork, a wheelbarrow, stood in front of him on the workbench. Longalio stared at it, head to one side, lost in a reverie, smiling to himself.

'That's a bonny thing.'

'Oh Calamorica.' He clutched his chest. 'I wish you

wouldn't do that. You nearly frightened the life out of me. What are you doing here?'

'I was bored and all by myself in Long Hall. I decided to go for a ramble through the wall. Why have you made a wheelbarrow?'

'I thought it would be useful for carting my finds back from the farm tip.'

'Seems like work for work's sake to me. Still, I suppose if you think it's worthwhile . . . '

'I'm so glad you like it,' he said, determined not to let his sister dampen his enthusiasm. 'I found the wheel on a broken toy. It's plastic, er, with a genuine rubber tyre,' he explained. 'The body's made of slats from a tomato box. I formed the handles from some bits of copper tube left by the Tallun who fixes the farm water pipes.'

'You don't have to sell it to me. Going to paint it?'

'Of course. Red, I think.'

'Red? Red?' she spluttered, looking at him in amazement, 'the last thing we need to be is conspicuous. It's why we all wear clothes to blend in with the grasses and leaves, remember? You want to paint your wheelbarrow - red?'

'Well, I could paint it grey, I suppose.'

'Grey? Dark brown, I think.'

'Dark brown?'

'Dark brown. All of it. And that includes the wheel with the genuine rubber tyre.'

'Right.'

Certain she'd prevented a disaster, Calamorica left Longalio to his work. She ambled off out of his workshop and down a passageway in the wall, in search of others in need of help or advice. When he was certain his sister had gone, he burst out laughing.

'Red?   Red?' he muttered, mimicking her voice perfectly. He opened his tin of paint, took up his brush and began painting his wheelbarrow dark brown.

*

Dorcan emerged from the wall, a mug in his hand. He was brushing his teeth with a willow twig and humming a lively Clyke tune. Sabrax was already outside, sitting on a three-legged oak stool in the bright, early morning sunshine. Dorcan took a mouthful of water, gargled musically with it and blew it out in a fine spray through a gap in his teeth. He slipped the willow twig into the top pocket of his coat.

'Nothing like clean teeth,' he said, running his finger over his gums. He put the mug down. 'A new staff?'

'Mmm.'

'Where's your old one?'

'Haven't you heard? I smashed it, staff-fighting with Rosmanda. I thought you would have heard about it by now.'

'Ye-e-es, should have heard of it, shouldn't I?' Dorcan put his hand to his chin and had a good think - why hadn't he been told about the broken staff? He liked to be kept informed about the daily happenings around the wall, as he was innately curious, or as some of the others put it, plain nosy. 'What is it you're carving?'

'Caripor Clyke defeating the Grosix of Alnur.'

'The Grosix? Now there was a monster.'

'Caripor. Now there was a Clyke.'

'You're right. What a brave Clyke he was. I don't think

I could have defeated the Grosix.'

'Nonsense. You're a brave little Clyke. I think you would have given of your best against it.'

Sabrax brushed the wood chips and shavings from his shirt and trousers with his hand.

'D'you think so?'

'Yes I do.'

'Thanks. Nice of you to say it.'

'Where are you off to?'

'Big Field.' Dorcan raised his foot up onto a stone to deal with a loose bootlace. 'See how the cabbages are doing. Make sure the hares haven't eaten them all.' He tied the lace quickly, lowered his foot and stamped his boot on the ground. 'See you later.'

Dorcan walked away and disappeared into the grasses.

'Take care,' Sabrax shouted after him, knowing that this was rather an optimistic wish, for his brother seemed to attract trouble to him like brambles to a sheep fleece.

After he'd finished the last fragment of detail, Sabrax blew away the dust and held the staff out at arm's length.

'That's not bad at all.'

'What's not bad?' asked Calamorica, who had slipped silently out of the wall.

'This.' Sabrax held his new staff aloft. He glanced up at his mother, silhouetted, her back to the sun. He shielded his eyes with his free hand for a moment and saw that she carried a water pail.

'Oh my. What a bonny thing. I wonder if I'll get a new staff for my birthnight?'

'Only if you're good.'

'You've always been a fine carver, ever since you were little. You get it from your grandfather.'

'The swallows have young ones already,' he said, 'I saw them yesterday, perched on the purlins in the old mill.'

He picked up a strand of dried horsetail rush and rubbed his staff vigorously with it, smoothing it off.

'Well, well, well. A flock of baby swallows. All the distance the birds have to travel, just to raise young here. Who'd be a swallow?' She held up her pail. 'I must go and get my water.'

Sabrax carried on working. He wiped the staff all over with beeswax then polished it with an old duster. He stood up, peered at the handle for a moment, and swiftly ran through a sequence of fighting moves, swinging the staff about over his head, before striding forward, jabbing the air.

'Oh yes.' He balanced his staff upright on one finger. 'Perfect.'

Pleased with his morning's work, he leaned his new staff against the wall, moved his stool out of the way and knelt down on the ground. With his willow-twig brush, he began to sweep up the remaining wood shavings.

'It's going to be a good day,' he said cheerfully.

The words had hardly left his lips when out of the corner of his eye he saw a flash of grey hurtle out of the wood. Sabrax knew instinctively what it was. He turned and looked for Calamorica. She was still on her way to the well and was out in open ground.

'Blood and sand, no,' he whispered. He saw for the first time that his mother was wearing her bonnet.

'Hawk,' screeched the little owl, perched in a nearby tree, 'watch out. Hawk. Watch out.'

Calamorica heard the owl's warning cries. She turned, dropped her pail and began to run as fast as she could, back towards the wall.

'Mother,' shouted Sabrax, 'run.'

'Watch out. Watch out. Run,' screeched the little owl, flapping his wings wildly.

Krokr was flying barely two feet off the ground now. Calamorica stumbled and fell, but got quickly to her feet again. Too late. Krokr stretched out his legs and feet and struck. Sabrax saw the flash of Krokr's sharp talons as he took Calamorica. She was plucked up, fought furiously, struggled from Krokr's grip and fell to the ground. Krokr flew off with only her bonnet clenched tightly in his foot. Sabrax ran straight to Calamorica. Out of nowhere, jagged forks of lightning flashed. Thunder rumbled. A great wind suddenly began to blow and hailstones fell out of a darkening sky. All was noise and confusion at the base of the wall. Other Clykes came out from gaps between the stones and went to help Sabrax. He had managed to get Calamorica in an upright position by now and held her steady. The hailstones grew larger. They danced about over the ground.

'Are you all right?'

'Wha. . . ?' wheezed Calamorica, who was clearly in shock.

'Come on,' Sabrax shouted to the others, 'let's get her inside.'

A stretcher was brought out. Sabrax and Longalio lifted Calamorica up and lowered her carefully down onto it. The Clykes carried Calamorica into the wall and straight through to her bedroom. Outside, lightning flashed again and a peal of thunder that broke directly overhead shook the very stones of the wall.

'What . . . happened?'

'Not now, sister,' said Longalio.

Longalio and Durabito picked up Calamorica gently between them and laid her down on her bed. Longalio went across and drew the curtains. Some of the other Clykes arrived, bringing hot water. They wanted to stay, but Durabito shooed them out and closed the door. After he had washed the dust from Calamorica's face with a flannel, Longalio put a few drops of witch hazel lotion in her eyes. He rubbed salve into the deep lesions on the back of her neck. Durabito had mixed a willow sleeping draught in a cup and now held the cup to Calamorica's lips. She drank from it.

'I, er . . . ' whispered Calamorica.

'Not now,' said Longalio, 'rest for you.'

Thunder broke above the wall again. The stones in the wall vibrated and shook. Durabito and Longalio stopped what they were doing and gazed up at the ceiling. Fine dust poured in through gaps between the stones and rained down on the floor. They looked again to Calamorica. She had sunk back in her pillow. Within minutes she was breathing steadily.

'Asleep,' whispered Longalio.

'Rest is what she'll need,' said Durabito.

Durabito gathered up the potions and salves. Longalio threw the face towel over his shoulder. He picked up his bowl of water. Going quietly, the brothers left the bedside and went out of the room.

Sabrax stood by the front door, watching the hail. Durabito and Longalio joined him.

'How is she?'

'She's asleep,' said Longalio.

'What a start to the day,' muttered Durabito.

'At least she's not dead, or hawk food,' said Sabrax, 'never really took it in that she was wearing her bonnet.' He gestured with open hands. 'My thoughts were on what I was doing.'

The three Clykes stared as hailstones, some the size of robin eggs, fell from the sky and gathered on the ground in front of their wall.

'I've not seen hail like this before,' said Durabito, 'have you?'

'No. Never in all my days,' said Longalio, 'I still can't come to terms with her wearing the talisman - and walking out across open ground.'

'Things will go downhill rapidly here until we get our brooch back,' said Durabito, a grim expression on his face, 'you'll see.'

*

Led by the swallows, a great flock of birds of all sizes and sorts mobbed Krokr Longtoe. There were so many, it seemed as though the hawk towed a small black cloud. Krokr twisted and turned violently through the air as he flew, showing his tormentors a taloned foot occasionally, in an attempt to drive them off. His efforts were in vain, for the flock stayed the course, flying hard after him. Krokr headed out over a great lake. It was here that the songbirds dropped out of the chase, reluctant to cross such a wide expanse of water. As Krokr flew on towards Mailcann, the only birds finally left in pursuit were the swallows, each one calling out in alarm as it flew. The intrepid birds did not turn back, but followed the great hawk as it darted among the trees and went deep into the forest, intent on following.

*

Outside, the violent storm raged. In Long Hall, Durabito, Longalio and Sabrax sat together. The carved casket lined with red velvet lay open on the table in front of them. It was empty.

'Absolute disaster,' muttered Sabrax.

He leapt up and walked across to the window.

'Catastrophic. Unbelievable. We all have to be so careful, our lives depend on it.'

Longalio and Durabito gave each other a sidelong glance. Longalio put a finger to his lips. Sabrax stared out of the window to where the tall birches stood, the trees bending in the gale.

'I've lost count of the number of times I've complained about the casual way in which my mother regarded the brooch,' said Sabrax, 'she'd grown complacent, wearing it almost daily. I can't help but think of her tale about the Clyke family who lost their talisman to a company of Roadwalkers in a game of chance. How their Tallun, a good Tallun, had died suddenly. His farm sold on to another Tallun who'd brought in double the number of milking cows and drained the land of its goodness. He ceased growing crops entirely. And in the end his farm had failed. Finally the whole Clyke family perished, killed when their wall collapsed during a winter storm. Now it's our brooch that's gone.'

He fell silent. Longalio and Durabito looked at each other again.

'My mother has made her mistake,' he said, turning to

face his uncles, 'and it cannot be undone. It's action that's needed. I'm sorry . . . for shouting so.'

Sabrax walked back to the table. He picked up the wooden box, stared at it for a moment, and snapped it shut.

'We'll find the hawk. Recover the brooch.'

'We don't even know where it is,' said Longalio.

'Perhaps Cataporinganio can help us,' said Durabito, 'cast a spell or something? He's co . . .'

'No,' said Sabrax, 'we mustn't approach him. We can't. He mustn't learn of this, understand? Imagine if word got out from this dale that we are incapable of protecting our talisman? If other tribes found out, well, it'd be shameful. We'd be a byword for carelessness. Can you imagine it? Can you? Laughed at by the other tribes? The humiliation we'd suffer. A storyteller from the Cardt, the Boskr, the Elor, or, dare I say it, the Foskyr, destroying our good name, in verse?'

As they talked, a great stone fell down inside the wall and flattened the stove. The three Clykes went across and stared at this fresh disaster.

'We won't be able to repair that,' said Durabito, 'flat as a cowpat.'

'Our talisman,' said Longalio, 'we've got to get it back. If we don't, well, who knows what will become of us?'

*

Rosmanda stood at the front door watching forks of lightning flashing overhead, to be followed almost immediately by a rolling clap of thunder. She fixed Sabrax with a determined look as he appeared.

40

'Sabs . . . '

'Can you do me a favour?'

'About the brooch . . . '

'Not now, Ros, please? Lot to think about at the moment.'

'I need you to listen to . . . '

'Will you find Dorcan for me?'

'You don't understand, I want to go . . . '

'He's out on Big Field.'

'I know that you and I . . .'

'Can you go and fetch him?'

'Oh, what's the use. It's like talking to a dandelion. Right, I'm on my way.'

*

Cataporinganio stared at his hand mirror and saw pictured there a great storm that raged in the dale where the Clykes lived.

'What a violent thunderstorm, most unusual. Such intensity. I wonder what on earth can have provoked it? Never mind. Let's see what I can do.'

Cataporinganio drew his hand over the mirror and concentrated hard.

'Camabalambolonga,' he whispered.

The raging storm displayed in his mirror stopped instantly, the sun appearing from behind the dark, retreating clouds. 'Ah, that's it. That's better. Give some fine days for my visit.'

He slid his hand mirror back into a pocket in his robe.

*

'The price of carelessness,' said Sabrax, pacing up and down outside Long Hall, 'blood and sand, it is.'

Sabrax looked out of the front door. The dark clouds were gone, the storm having passed as suddenly as it had arrived. Now the sun was shining.

'All this going on as I'm quietly picking caterpillars off cabbage leaves,' muttered Dorcan, 'it's an absolute nightmare.'

Dorcan glanced at Sabrax and saw plainly that he was distraught.

'The feather and red jewel together, they'd look like an injured bird to the hawk.'

'She shouldn't have been wearing it out in the open.'

'I know. I'm making excuses for our mother.'

'Yes you are.'

'Well, what are we going to do, Sabs?'

'Two things. First, we must find out where the hawk has gone. I think the swallows will be able to help us with that.'

'And the second?'

'Wherever it is, we've got to go after it. Find the brooch - bring it home.'

'So that's the plan then, is it?'

'That's the plan.'

*

Chapter Four

It was late morning when the swallows returned and they bore bad news.

'The swallows followed the hawk all the way to its nest in a tree,' said Sabrax, 'watched it land and saw that the bonnet was locked tight in the hawk's foot. The hawk waited until its talons fell open, then attacked the bonnet. It tore the feather off with its beak.'

'What for?'

'Rage, fury. Hawks are like that.'

'I see,' said Dorcan, looking worried.

'Then it tossed the bonnet aside. That's what they said.'

'Where is the hawk's nest?'

'Mailcann Forest.'

'I feel ill.' Dorcan sighed deeply. He thought about the many clear evenings when he had stood on a wall top and looked out with a sense of foreboding towards Mailcann Forest, dark on a distant skyline.

'You remember the stories we were told when we were little, Sabrax? About the Clykes who travelled there?'

'Of course I do.'

'And how they never came back.'

'Some did, surely.'

'No, none did. It's a brave Clyke who'd go there of his own accord.'

'We're brave aren't we?'

'If you say so.' Unconvinced, Dorcan shook his head.

'Go and tell the swallows of our intentions.'

'What are our intentions?'

'To journey to Mailcann,' said Sabrax, 'meet the swallows there, they'll show us the tree. We'll retrieve our talisman and bring it home safely.'

'Just like that?'

'Just like that.'

By lunchtime, there was a distinct sense of purpose about the brothers, for they had sorted out the equipment they would need for their journey. Spike-shod tree-climbing boots had been wrapped and packed in their bags, along with their tree axes. A change of clothing, packets of food and bottles of dandelion tea filled the remaining space in the bags. Two lengths of baling twine had been wound into coils and lay ready. Sabrax and Dorcan filled the mustard pouches on their belts with fresh mustard powder: a handful cast in the face of a stoat or a fox could save a Clyke from a brutal death. At long last, Dorcan and Sabrax slung the coils of line over their shoulders, picked up their bags and walked out of the wall.

'Now look confident, for their sake,' said Sabrax.

'Understood.'

The two Clykes strolled down to the foot of the wall

where the others stood waiting for them.

'Well, that hawk's got a surprise coming to it,' shouted Dorcan, pausing for a second for effect, 'me and Sabrax.'

Dorcan held his fist in the air as the Clykes clapped and whistled. Sabrax strode forward and stood in the middle of the group.

'Come on, cheer up, everything's going to be all right, you'll see. You've got to convince Dorcan and me that while we're away, you can all act as though nothing has happened. Uncle Durabito and Uncle Longalio, make sure everybody is kept safe until we return.'

'We will,' said Durabito, shaking Sabrax's hand, 'we'll not let you down.'

'Ready?'

Dorcan nodded and shook his fist again.

'Tell our mother not to worry,' said Sabrax to Durabito, 'we'll be back soon. Look after her, don't forget to make a fuss, and stop her feeling guilty.'

'What about her birthnight?'

'Help her to celebrate it.'

'I've something to tell you.'

Durabito shuffled his feet and his eyes were downcast. Sabrax could see he was struggling.

'Go on.'

'I've invited Cataporinganio to Calamorica's birthnight.'

'I see.'

'I organised it all before this disaster happened.'

'I've never met the great wizard, Uncle Durabito: Cataporinganio, a living wonder. It's too late to do anything about it now. Be strong. Let him come. After she gets over the initial shock, I'm sure my mother will be delighted to see him. Not a word to him about the loss of our talisman, though, or our journey. I've heard he's skilled in asking wheedling questions.'

'No one will say a thing,' said Durabito, 'I promise you. Go safely and come back soon.'

Sabrax and Dorcan gathered up their climbing lines and bags. Loud cheering rose up from the rest of the Clykes and some tossed their caps high into the air. The two Clykes walked off from their wall, went among the tall grasses and vanished.

Clouds covered the sun and a cooling wind blew. It was a perfect afternoon for walking - walking warily and keeping under cover of the plants. Sabrax and Dorcan crossed field after field in the valley bottom, bobbing under gates, slipping through hogg holes and going through gaps in fallen walls. Some of the fields were filled with tall hay, the breeze bending and swishing the stalks. Other fields were given over to clover and echoed to the loud hum of bees about their work. Crops of oats filled even more fields, their light green heads ripening in the summer warmth. When they arrived at a field on a south-west facing slope, the brothers were surprised to find that haytiming was finished there, the bare yellow-green field smelling of earth and dotted with hay bales. A party of rooks moved over the ground, bills prodding the long narrow lines of hay that had been missed by the baling machine.

Soon the two Clykes had left the fields of the lower dale behind and now negotiated a steep track that emerged from a field gate at Fell End and ran up the fell side. When they saw that the track cut back across the contour, away from the direction in which they travelled, the two Clykes left it, following instead a well-worn sheep trod that looked as though it might lead on to the broad tops. Halfway up the trod, the pair slowed and stopped for a moment. In the distance, the green, rounded domes of unknown hills stood up under an anvil shaped mass of grey-white cloud. They'd hoped to stay in sight of the river that ran down their dale, but saw that it swung away westwards in a great loop, to vanish into the distance. For the next part of their journey they would turn east and follow the fell walls that would lead them to Mailcann.

The brothers continued walking, their initial eagerness fading with every step that led them further away from home. They talked less and less until, eventually, they travelled in silence. Both thought about the enormity of the undertaking, every so often their progress punctuated by a large sigh. The sheep trod joined a wide track of crushed stone that zigzagged up from the valley bottom. It, too, seemed to lead on to the tops. The pair followed it as it wound among huge lumps of jagged, shattered rock and hills of spoil that scarred the landscape. They came to a wooden gate fixed between two rock outcrops. The gate was closed over the track and secured with a rusty chain and padlock. Barbed wire had been bound around the top bar. They saw that the track only ran down into an abandoned quarry far below.

'It's a dead end,' said Sabrax.

Fixed to the gate was a faded notice. Dorcan stared at the upraised hand on it and held his own hand up in imitation. The bold red letters, "Danger. Quarry Workings. Keep Out" had no meaning for him, as Clykes did not speak or understand Tallun.

'We'll have to go along there,' said Sabrax, pointing to a narrow rock sill skirting the rim of the quarry.

'Can't we go back and find another way?'

'It would take too long. I reckon it'll get us to the other side,' said Sabrax determinedly, 'then we can pick up that path.'

He pointed to a distinct path that snaked away up a slope above the quarry and on towards the fell top.

'You all right, Dorcs?'

'Yeherrss. Bit worried, you know.'

The two Clykes got to their knees and crawled under the gate.

'Concentrate and watch how you go,' said Sabrax, a note of seriousness in his voice now. 'Can't make a mistake in here. It would be fatal.'

Sabrax and Dorcan began their traverse of the quarry edge, trying not to look down. A series of giant steps in the rock, cut by the Talluns as they won the stone, rose up from the quarry floor. Each step had its own sheer face with many narrow ledges on which gulls, crows and jackdaws perched.

'Never seen so many birds in one place,' said Dorcan.

Out of nowhere came the vibrating rasp of wind through feathers. Sabrax and Dorcan froze. Two peregrine falcons tore across the quarry face below, screaming loudly. Suddenly the whole bird population in the quarry erupted from the ledges and filled the air. One of the peregrines took a bird in flight. Chacking loudly, a great flock of jackdaws flew up over the quarry rim. Wings flapped in the two Clykes' faces. The draught plucked at them. The clamour deafened them. They could see nothing through the noisy, swirling flock.

Dorcan lost his footing and lurched forward. Sabrax grabbed out, seized a handful of shirt and pulled hard.

'I've got you. I've got you.'

Dorcan was inched back from the edge. He was shaking. The falcons were gone as quickly as they had appeared, the mass of birds wheeling about in the air, folding their wings and landing again on the ledges. The din subsided. The alarm was over.

It was an hour later when Sabrax and Dorcan stood below the fell top at the end of their arduous climb.

'That was hard going,' said Sabrax, wiping his forehead with the back of his hand.

'Not the way I'd have come, given the choice,' said a breathless Dorcan.

They trudged the last few yards up onto the very top and were met by the astounding sight of a circle of tall stones. The two Clykes stood before them in silence, overawed. He did not know why, but there was something about the place that resonated immediately with Sabrax, this huge silent stone circle set out on a wide plateau surrounded by hills. He and Dorcan ambled among the monoliths.

'Are we the first Clykes to see them?'

'They seem familiar to me,' said Sabrax, 'yet I've never been here before.'

'Who d'you think put them up?'

'Not the work of us Clykes, that's certain.'

'I wonder how long they've been here.'

'They look as though they've been here forever,' said Sabrax.

'Just look at the size of them.'

'Must be twenty times our height - or more.'

'But why are they here?' asked Dorcan.

'That's something only the stones could tell us. But on midwinter morning what do we look for?'

'The sun rising between the figures on the hill?'

'Look back the way we've come. Down in the valley bottom, you should be able to see our farm. Go on, up you go. Have a look.'

Dorcan threw down his bag and line and began to climb up the tallest stone. Sabrax ran his hand over the smooth face of one of the other blue-grey stones. He drew it away instantly. He stared first at the stone and then at his hand. Dorcan, meanwhile, had reached the top and gazed down into the dale.

'You're right, my but you're right, Sabrax. I can see our farm from here. There's the hay barn and the farmhouse and the workshop and the orchard and the mere. These are the figures on the hill.'

Dorcan turned round and stared out towards the tall trees of Mailcann Forest. 'The forest still looks a long way off.'

'It comes nearer with every stride.'

'I mean it still *looks* a long way off.' Dorcan scrambled back down.

Sabrax touched the stone again with his finger.

'Wharr!'

'What's up?'

'Something went through me,' said Sabrax, 'something tingly.'

'From a stone?'

'From that stone, anyway. Let's have a rest and something to drink. We need one after all that effort.

There'll be somewhere safe nearby.'

'What's wrong with here?' said Dorcan.

'Sit out in the open? All kinds of wild animals roaming about - and hawks?'

'Hawks? Great badger beards. Will the hawk be up here?'

Sabrax pointed to a tiny speck, black against the white cloud, high in the sky.

'That could be it.'

The two Clykes scurried out of the stone circle and ran on through the tall grasses. They came to a clump of gorse bushes, went in among them and sat down. Sabrax opened the flap on his bag, fished around inside and got out a bottle of cold tea. After taking a mouthful himself, he handed it to Dorcan who, without prompting, took several glugs.

'Can't beat cold tea. Nothing like a drop of cold tea for quenching a thirst.' Dorcan pushed the cork stopper into the mouth of the bottle and returned it to Sabrax. 'Nothing like a drop of cold tea,' he said again, wiping his mouth with the back of his sleeve. He belched.

'Little piglet.'

'I'm not! So how far would you say it is to Mailcann?'

'Not so far now. Not so far.'

The two Clykes rested. Dorcan stretched out, his bag a pillow for his head. Sabrax, his head cradled on his knees, gazed at the stone circle. Dorcan started snoring.

'Come on, don't settle down, let's get the strides going again,' said Sabrax, shaking him.

'Wha . . . what?'

Sabrax stood up. He swung his bag and climbing line over his shoulder. He looked at Dorcan who had got to his feet and now struggled with twists in his bag strap.

'I don't know. How have you managed to get to the age you are?'

'Not usually a problem, bag straps.'

Sabrax straightened his strap.

'There, that's it, that's better. I look quite smart, don't you think?' Dorcan shrugged his shoulders and puffed out his chest. 'I'm ready for anything now. Well almost anything.'

*

Longalio and Durabito sat together in their armchairs by the fire in Long Hall sipping their mugs of dandelion tea.

'I'm concerned,' confided Longalio.

'We all are.'

'No, I mean concerned - about not having made, er, contingencies.'

'Eh?' Durabito looked quizzically at him.

'We've got to make alternative arrangements - should Sabrax and Dorcan - er, you know.'

'What?'

'If anything should befall them and they don't er, get back, in one piece as it were.'

'See what you mean,' said Durabito, 'in case something - happens.'

'Mmmm.'

'Make preparations for - other Clykes - to go and try and recover the brooch?'

'Mmmm. That sort of thing.'

'It would be the responsible thing to do.'

'Yes it would,' said Longalio, nodding.

'But who to send? That's the question.'

Longalio and Durabito looked at each other.

'We are needed here,' said Durabito, 'to look after things. It's what Sabrax said.'

'That's right.'

'Look after things until he and Dorcan return.'

'Until they return,' said Longalio.

They looked at each other again.

*

The sun had almost set; its final rays fretted the trees and hedges in the landscape and cast long shadows over the ground. Narrow bands of high cloud streaked the horizon, their edges turned dusky pink. The first evening star had appeared in a still-blue sky. It shone with a faint light. Sabrax and Dorcan stopped beside a beck. The brothers pulled their bags off their shoulders and laid them flat on the ground.

'We've done well, haven't we?'

'Far better than I thought we would.'

'My feet are on fire,' complained Dorcan, pulling off his boots.

For most of the afternoon, the two Clykes had set up a fast walking pace. Many new and intriguing landmarks had been observed, discussed and left behind. They'd played spot the flower as they walked, with double points for wild roses. Then it was spot the bird, treble points for summer visitors. When they'd grown tired of this, they talked about different kinds of knots and when to use them. Frogs were talked about next; how they hibernated in mud underwater throughout the winter and were still alive in spring. Then they ranked from one to fifty the best meals they'd ever eaten. Evening was approaching when general weariness had set in and their leg muscles had shown the first signs of cramp. It was during a deep debate about whether it was possible to make jam from grass that the conversation had suddenly turned to where to find shelter for the night.

'How far would you say it is to the forest now?' asked Dorcan, rubbing his tired feet with a handful of soothing dock leaf.

'I reckon if we walk like we have today, we'll get there tomorrow.'

Dorcan thought this must be true, for of all the Clykes his brother was easily the best reckoner.

'Exciting, eh?'

'Ye-hearrr-sssss.' Dorcan yawned loudly. 'Exciting.'

Sabrax opened the flap on his bag, put in his hand and felt around inside. He took out a couple of packets of food and his bottle of tea. Dorcan had finished rubbing his feet with the dock leaves and now sat on the ground twisling his toes.

'Funny things - toes. And feet.'

'They smell a bit,' said Sabrax playfully, pinching his nose with his fingers.

'Never.' Dorcan folded up his socks and stowed them in his bag.

'I'm glad they're your feet and not mine.'

The two Clykes lay stretched out on the ground in the afterglow of sunset, eating their supper.

'The sky's big,' said Dorcan, pointing to it with the tip of his sandwich.

'It is. We only see a small part of it where we live, certainly makes you think.'

'Yes, it does. Wonder what else there is we don't normally see?'

As the evening darkened, more and more stars appeared. A three-quarter moon began its climb up into the night sky.

'I'm tired,' Dorcan yawned.

'Me too. One of these might be empty.'

Sabrax gestured over his shoulder with his thumb to rabbit holes in a bank. Dorcan got up and strolled across to them. He went into one.

'Well?'

'Just the job. Bone dry. It'll do for us.'

Sabrax gathered up their things and followed Dorcan into the hole. Their bags had been designed to double as sleeping sacks. Once they'd been emptied of their contents, the brothers only had to pull out a large folded flap from inside the bag, undo a couple of ties, give the bag a vigorous shake and there it was - a sleeping sack. For pillows they used their boots and coils of line. Sabrax and Dorcan quickly emptied theirs, shook them out, wriggled in and settled down. They lay there in silence.

'D'you think the hawk would be able to sleep if it knew we were on our way?' said Dorcan suddenly, yawning loudly, 'do you? Hey? Sabrax? Asleep, fast asleep. Didn't even say goodnight.'

*

Chapter Five

Clykes filed into Long Hall and gathered around the big table where Calamorica sat alone eating breakfast. She knew it was her birthnight tonight, but really didn't feel like celebrating anything.

'What are you lot staring at? Hmmm? Something else gone disastrously wrong?'

'Look at your night stones,' said Durabito.

A large glass jar filled to the brim with small pebbles stood on the table and next to it was a single pebble.

'A single night stone,' said Calamorica, in feigned astonishment, struggling to keep her sadness deep inside, 'that means it must be . . . '

'Your birthnight tonight,' exclaimed Durabito, 'two hundred summers.'

She leaned across, dropped the night stone into the jar and then tipped out all the stones onto the table.

'Oh dear,' she whispered, 'another year starts tomorrow. Don't think I can face another year.'

'We've a surprise for you,' said Durabito.

'A surprise? For me?'

'A special visitor,' continued Durabito, 'coming to help you celebrate your birthnight. Someone you haven't seen in ages.'

'Who's organised this?'

'I have,' said Durabito.

There were three peals of thunder, one after the other.

'Come along everybody,' ordered Durabito, 'I think our guest has arrived.'

The Clykes rushed outside and gathered in a circle at the foot of the wall. They all stared up at the sky.

'What are we looking for?' asked Calamorica, pushing in among them.

'A raven,' replied Durabito.

'Oh no,' muttered Calamorica, 'by the horns of Bador, no. Not him.'

Thunder clapped and rolled again.

'There it is,' said Rosmanda, who had the sharpest eyes of all the Clykes. She pointed to a black speck high in the sky.

The speck grew into a blob.

'It's coming down,' said Rosmanda.

Now the Clykes could all see that it was, indeed, a raven. Soon the bird flew in a wide circle over their heads, its glossy black plumage shining in the bright sunlight. The raven called out loudly.

'Pruuk, pruuk.'

It folded its wings, dropped from the sky and fell towards earth like a great sharp black stone. The Clykes turned away and could not look, for they expected the bird to be dashed on the ground. But the raven extended its wings at the last possible moment, came out of its stoop and landed on the wall top.

'What a fantastic bit of flying,' said Durabito.

'Not bad,' said Longalio, 'but compared with the peregrine, well . . . '

He tailed off and shrugged his shoulders.

'Pruuk, pruuk,' the bird called again and bowed its large head.

The raven leapt from the wall top to land on the ground in a flutter of wings. There was a sudden flash of light. The Clykes shielded their eyes with their hands. When they looked again, the raven had vanished and in its place stood a most unusual looking Clyke who appeared to glow. He wore a cape the colour of new leaves, with strange symbols and devices woven into collar and hem. It was slung back over his shoulder. His coat, shirt and trousers were extraordinary and made from the finest silk. On his feet the Clyke sported a pair of fine brown canvas boots.

'Cataporinganio,' whispered Calamorica under her breath, 'all we need. He's the last one I'd wish to see at this awful time.'

'Calamorica Clyke. Har, har. How are you?' shouted Cataporinganio, his voice booming around the walls.

'I, er, I'm all right.'

'All right? It's not good enough. I want you to be - overjoyed.'

'Er, I am, really. It's such a surprise seeing you, after so long a time.'

'I know what you mean. I always have this effect on others, can't help it of course, all part and parcel of being such an amazing wizard.'

The two old friends wrapped their arms about each

other and danced a little jig, the Clykes assembled there clearly amazed to see normally grumpy Calamorica behave like this.

'I am Cataporinganio. I sing perfect songs,' he proclaimed, walking among the Clykes. 'Tonight we shall honour Calamorica Clyke on the occasion of her birthnight. Anyone found not enjoying themselves will be turned into - a spi-der.'

He held one cupped hand over the other and whispered strange words. He raised a hand to reveal a large black spider lying in his palm. He threw the spider into the air. It turned into a puff of smoke. The Clykes whistled and applauded.

The wizard walked about in front of the Clykes. All eyes were fixed on him as, with a flourish of his hand, he drew a bonnet out of thin air. Clykes whistled and applauded again. Cataporinganio smiled as he produced a fine gold ring from thin air with his other hand.

'Happy birthnight, Calamorica.'

He handed the bonnet and ring to her. She pulled on the bonnet. It was a perfect fit.

'A new bonnet,' she said, with a forced smile, 'just what I need.'

Calamorica slid the ring onto her finger and it, too, fitted perfectly. Clykes clapped loudly and their enthusiastic whistles gave way to heartfelt cheers. One of the Clykes started to chant their names and the others took it up.

'Cata-porin-ganio, Calam-orica, Cata-porin-ganio, Calam-orica.'

'They like you,' said Calamorica.

'They like us.'

Cataporinganio raised his hand in acknowledgement of the Clykes' welcome. The two old friends put their arms around each other again and wandered off with their names ringing in their ears.

Longalio walked into the kitchen. He had baked a cake for Calamorica's birthnight the previous evening, when the people at the farmhouse were asleep. Now he got out an old, well-fingered cookery book and placed it on the table. He studied it, turning the pages rapidly as he sought a particular recipe.

'Toppings, toppings, where are you, toppings?'

He continued to turn the pages and then stopped.

'Ah. Here we are. Toppings. Betrothal cake, no. Summer cake, no. Birthnight cake, ah that's it, that's the one. Well, well, well. This recipe's Risana Clyke's - Calamorica's grandmother. There's a thing.'

Longalio stood the book up against a mixing bowl and laid a wooden spoon on the page to mark the place.

'I'll leave that there, ready for later.'

He ambled across into the pantry and picked up the cake.

'Now. Where to put it? Somewhere out of sight. Away from prying eyes and little fingers, I think. Ah, up here.' He reached up and placed the cake on the sill of the high window, which was open. 'There, that's it.'

*

Sabrax and Dorcan walked in the early morning on a track that crossed a vast, open expanse of moorland beneath a giant sky. It was all so very different from the rich flat soils of the farmland where they lived. There the walls and hedges and woods bound them in. Up here there were only twisted thorns with their roots in peat, and extensive blankets of heather. The piercing cries of unknown birds came on a wind that whined through thorns and shook the heather stalks. The brothers paused for a moment by a narrow trail that crossed the track on which they walked.

They studied the fresh animal prints in the soil.

'Fox.' Sabrax pointed to the russet-coated killer's distinctive paw prints. 'There's always a fox.'

'Look. Badger.' Dorcan pointed to a set of larger paw prints. 'And deer, too. It's well-use . . .'

Sabrax clamped his hand around Dorcan's mouth and dragged him down into the heather.

'What are you doing?' hissed Dorcan, through Sabrax's fingers.

Sabrax put a finger to his lips and pointed to a hawk high up in the sky. The bird was soaring on thermals rising from the warm earth. Two crows were stooping and mobbing the hawk as it scanned the landscape, looking for prey. The bird had its tail buffeted by a crow beak. It turned in the air and showed the crow its feet. The second crow struck the hawk a blow on its wing tip with its bill. It lost a flight feather from its own wing for its trouble as the hawk retaliated with its sharp talons. The crows drew back as the hawk soared higher and higher.

From the depths of the heather, Sabrax and Dorcan had watched the crows mobbing the hawk. Now their eyes were fixed on the black crow feather as it spiralled to earth.

'I wonder if it's the hawk we are looking for?'

'It might be,' said Sabrax.

The hawk drew in its wings, went into a long-drawn-out stoop across the whole of the wide sky, and crashed into a clump of heather not far off. A loud squeal rose up.

'D'you think it's caught something?' said Dorcan.

'I would say so. Poor creature.'

It was late morning before the brothers stopped again. Their track had led them steeply down to a lower contour and now they stood beside a nest of large rocks by a small beck, staring at the remains of a sheep lying on the ground. The skeleton had been picked clean, the ragged fleece spread in a wide circle around the bones.

'Crows,' said Sabrax, 'know their work anywhere.'

'Nothing ever goes to waste, does it?'

'When there are crows about it doesn't. Let's have a rest.'

Sabrax led the way under the shade of a stand of ash trees. The two Clykes took off their boots and socks. They sat down on a large flat stone that overhung a small pool fed by the beck. It was pleasant sitting there, feet dipped in the cold running water, gazing out over a new dale. Below them the dry-stone walls gave way to hedges and ditches and beyond these, hundreds of buildings were laid out over the ground in circles and squares. Tall poles stood at intervals among them. Some of the big buildings had smaller buildings nearby. Narrow roads ran from among the buildings to one great wide road that snaked away down the valley. Four wheeled machines, similar to the ones on their farm, were moving in both directions on the big road.

'What do you make of it all?'

'Looks like a giant farm to me,' said Dorcan, 'what do you think?'

'Could be a giant farm, I suppose. It's a place where a lot of Talluns live, that's certain. Not something we've seen before.'

'I'll tell you something we have seen before.'

'What?'

'Food.'

'Only ever one thing on your mind,' said Sabrax.

Sabrax and Dorcan dried their feet with dock leaves and put on their socks and boots. Dorcan hurriedly undid the flap on his bag, took out his food, unwrapped it and began to eat straightaway.

'Make it last,' said Sabrax, 'we don't know how long we are going to be away.'

'You don't have to lecture me. I'm not a baby, you know.'

*

Chapter Six

Rosmanda had made a party hat out of willow wands for herself. Now she plaited coloured feathers into the brim.

'I hope it all goes well this evening,' said Rosmanda, holding her hat out at arm's length and pulling at the feathers.

'It'll be fine,' replied Woadica, busy wrapping a pair of new green boots in coloured paper, 'you'll see. Parties always get you going, don't you think? Pull you in.'

'Normally they do, yes, but how will mother feel about Sabrax and Dorcan not being there?'

'It's up to us to help take her mind off things. Just imagine what she's going through, what it must be like, knowing it was you who had lost the talisman.'

Rosmanda put on her party hat.

'What do you think?'

Woadica looked up and giggled.

'Oh, it's so funny.'

*

After they had finished eating, Sabrax and Dorcan gathered up their belongings, pulled their bags and lines over their shoulders and set off again. It wasn't long before they were back into their stride. New landscape features that appeared at every turning in the track were studied and discussed. But their rambling conversations only masked their real concerns; nagging, doubting, inner voices whispered away as they walked. Sabrax pondered on whether their quest would be successful. Would everything work out well? Would he and Dorcan survive? Dorcan wondered if his food would last out.

Sabrax, as he strolled along, ran a twig on the grass stalks and it click, click, clicked. He was soon lost in the hypnotic spell of the clump of his boots on the ground and the click of the twig on the stalks. It was only after the grasses alongside the track ended and the clicking stopped that he came out of his reverie. Sabrax turned and looked back. Dorcan had gone.

'Dorcan. Dorcan? Where are you? Stop messing about. Dor-can. Dor-can.'

Sabrax quickly retraced his steps, following his footprints there in the soft ground. He came to the place where Dorcan's prints deviated from his own and went off to the left, towards a wall. Sabrax followed them. When he got to the wall, he saw that a small tunnel had been built into it at ground level, leading to the next field. A wooden board was set in the ground in front of the opening. Lying in a heap beside it were Dorcan's bag and coil of line. Of Dorcan there was no sign. Sabrax knelt down and picked up the bag.

'Blood and sand what's he gone and done now. Has something got him? A stoat? A fox? What?'

He stood up.

'Dor-can. Dor-can.'

'I'm here,' came the faint reply.

Sabrax listened intently as he looked about. He shouted again.

'Dorcan. Dorcan.'

'Here. I'm in here. Help.'

Sabrax looked down, certain that the faint cry came from beneath the wooden board.

'Are you under there, Dorcan?'

'Of-course-I-am,' came the peevish reply, 'it's a trap.'

'What are you doing in there?'

'What do you think I'm doing? I'm trapped, of course.'

Sabrax put his foot on the front of the board and pushed down gently. The board sank, before rocking back up again.

'On a pivot,' he muttered.

Trying not to step on the board, he clambered through the opening to the rear of the trap. He looked around for a suitable stone for his purpose. He found one. He picked it up and dropped it on the back of the board; it sank down an inch, while the front of the board rose up. Sabrax knelt down and peered in through the gap.

'Hallooooo, Dorcan,' he said playfully, in a deep voice, 'what's that in there with you?'

'Never mind. Get me out of here will you? As fast as possible, please.'

Sabrax went to the back of the trap again. This time he found a very large round stone and pushing with all his might, managed to roll it to the board. He gave the stone a final shove. It fell onto the back of the board, jamming the trap open. Dorcan and the skeleton of a rabbit were revealed. Dorcan scrambled out. Sabrax came back through the opening.

'I saw the hole in the wall. Thought I'd go and have a look at it, see what was on the other side.' Dorcan beat the dust from his clothes.

'Keep together, stupid. Everyone expects me to get you home safely from this venture. I might not have found you. You could've died in there. Two skeletons, side by side.'

'But you did find me,' whispered Dorcan, 'and I'm very grateful.'

He raised his eyebrows, swung his bag and line over his shoulder and ran after Sabrax, who had already walked off.

*

It was mid afternoon on Calamorica Clyke's farm. Hens in the farmyard clucked in alarm and ran off in all directions, as a long brown stoat appeared from a hole in a gnarled tree root. The stoat ran across the farmyard and disappeared under the hen shed. The farm Tallun looked up from his work in the byre and stared out into the glare of the afternoon. He noticed nothing untoward and went back to his work.

The stoat's sleek head popped up at the threshold of the hen shed. The hens inside saw it and panicked. Several hens fluttered right past the stoat and escaped outside, clucking loudly. Other hens flapped up to the high perches under the roof eaves. Disturbed by the noise from the hens, the farm Tallun now left what he was doing and went to investigate. The stoat had already made its way into the laying boxes in the hen shed and was about to roll an egg out of a nest. A large stick wielded by the farm Tallun slammed down, missed the creature and broke the egg. The stoat leapt from the nest box, landed on the floor, wriggled out through a knothole, ran across the open ground and disappeared into a wall.

*

Longalio was back working in the kitchen. He'd put honey, cream and crushed flowers into a large white bowl. Now he was beating them together with a willow whisk. This was to be the topping for Calamorica's birthnight cake. He stopped whisking his mix and stared into space.

'Summertime, ah, summertime,' he muttered, 'swifts and swallows have returned, trees are in leaf and the days are so long. Lovely time of year. Now, ah, er, where was I? Ah, yes, the topping.'

He whisked the topping briskly again then dipped in his finger and tasted his creation.

'Mmmmmm. That's good. Now for the cake.'

He went across to the windowsill. The cake had gone.

'I know I put it there. I know I did,' he muttered, pulling a stool beneath the sill and climbing up.

The sill was indeed empty. Longalio poked his head out of the window and looked down. He saw a pile of crumbs next to the telltale tracks of the cake thief, a set of large paw prints in the loose soil at the base of the wall heading back to the farmhouse.

'Blast it. Pinched by the farm dog,' he shouted, 'I hope

the cake gives it indigestion. Too late to bake another. What on earth am I going to do?'

'Ahem.'

Longalio jumped. He spun round.

'Cataporinganio. I do wish others wouldn't keep doing that.'

'Doing what?'

'Creeping up on me,' he said in exasperation, getting down from the stool.

Cataporinganio stood beside the kitchen table.

'I'm sorry if I frightened you. I say, what a wonderful kitchen.'

'I made it. All of it: the utensils and the cupboards, worktops, table and chairs, all out of pieces of old wooden furniture and metal I got from the farm tip.'

'Magnificent. But what's troubling you? You look worried, Longalio.'

'I am. I'd baked a cake for Calamorica's birthnight and the blasted farm dog's stolen it.'

'Never mind. Let's see what I can do to help. Clear the table, will you. What kind of cake was it?'

'A fruit cake. I made it with the last of our dried fruit, flour and farm butter and eggs. Oh it was good, if I don't mind saying so myself. Cakes are what I'm best at. Well, that and joinery.'

'How big was this cake?'

'This big.' Longalio drew the cake's dimensions in the loose flour on the tabletop with his finger. 'And this thick.' He showed the thickness between his hands.

Cataporinganio pointed a finger at the table. He mumbled a few words under his breath. There was a brilliant flash of light and a loud whistling sound. A fruitcake materialised out of thin air on the tabletop.

'Like that?'

'Just like that,' said Longalio, his eyes wide. He picked up the cake and studied it closely.

'Better put the topping on. I know my cake won't taste as good as yours would have, but I'm sure it will suffice.'

*

Chapter Seven

Sabrax and Dorcan arrived at another wall on the far side of a broad field of barley.

'Let me climb this one,' begged Dorcan.

'Go on then.'

Dorcan scrambled up to the top of the wall in a matter of seconds and got to his feet among the camstones. He looked around.

'Sabrax,' he shouted, gesturing wildly with his arm, 'come up here and have a look at this.'

Sabrax scaled the wall speedily, moving nimbly from stone to stone. He clambered over the camstones and stood up beside Dorcan.

'Oh my,' said Sabrax.

The two Clykes gazed out at a great lake that occupied the bottom of a broad valley.

'Nobody told me we'd have a lake to cross,' said Dorcan.

On the far side of the water, the tall trees of Mailcann Forest rose up.

'So, the hawk's nest is somewhere in that lot,' said Dorcan, pointing.

'At the top of one of those trees.'

'At the top?'

'It's where they nest. At the very top.'

'Oh.'

The wall on which the brothers stood ran into the distance, then disappeared from view as it plunged away downhill towards the lake.

'What are we waiting for?' exclaimed Dorcan.

He leapt from the wall onto a branch of a nearby bush. As the branch bent under his weight, so it lowered him gently down to the ground. He let go of the branch. It sprang back violently.

'You could injure yourself doing that,' shouted Sabrax, climbing down steadily, 'then what would we do?'

'Sorry. I never thought,' Dorcan muttered, 'I do it all the time at home.'

'There would be dozens of us to help you at home if you're injured, but out here?'

Dorcan looked downcast. Sabrax saw this.

'Well? What are we waiting for? Let's go and have a look at the lake. Wahooo.' He ran off.

'Wahhoo,' shouted Dorcan, brightening up immediately and following him.

The two Clykes hurried along beside the base of the wall through a lush haymeadow, the tall grasses vying for sunspace with a host of flowers.

'Why's the lake there?'

'There's probably too much water for the river to cope with, I think,' said Sabrax.

'Like our mere?'

'Exactly. It just gathers.'

Soon the ground began to fall away, the dry-stone wall descending with the hill, to end abruptly at the lake. Sabrax and Dorcan, talking excitedly, stepped down the hill beside the wall and reached the gravel beach. They ran to the water's edge. Small waves rolled in and broke on the lakeshore.

'It's big, isn't it?'

'Big? It's vast,' said Dorcan.

The lake stretched left, right and in front of them, bounded in the distance by the dark mass of Mailcann Forest. There were small islands in the lake, each one covered in dense tree growth that grew right up to the edge of the water, obscuring their beaches, creating the illusion of floating woods.

'Are we the first Clykes to set eyes on the lake?'

'There were other Clykes who travelled here,' said Sabrax, 'but they, er, never, er . . .'

'Came back to tell the tale.'

'We will. We'll return home and tell the tale.'

'How are we going to get over to the other side?'

'Easy. Build a raft and paddle it across.'

'You think we can paddle a raft all the way over there?'

'That's it, little brother. We've built rafts before - on the mere.'

'Er, the mere's not quite as big as this. Or as deep.'

'Water's water to me. Six inches, six foot, sixty . . . '

'All right, I get the idea.'

Sabrax and Dorcan dropped their bags, got out their tree axes and went into a small wood above the beach. After sharpening the edge of his axe with a whetstone, Sabrax started work, quickly chopping small straight lengths from a fallen beech limb. He and Dorcan pulled them clear of the undergrowth and trimmed them with their axes. Soon a stack of poles had risen up.

'That should be enough,' said Sabrax, 'oh, and this for a pair of paddles.'

He threw out a short, thick log.

The two Clykes hauled the poles down to the shoreline and set them out on the beach in the shape of a raft. Sabrax returned to the wood. He looked for a young ivy clinging to a tree. He found one, cut it down and pulled it to the beach. Driving his axe spike into a tree stump, he used the sharp edge of the axe blade to slit the ivy into two long sinuous strips. Soon a pile of supple lashing lay coiled about his feet. While Sabrax had been working, Dorcan had split the short log in two with his axe and had fashioned a pair of paddles.

'What do you think?' he asked, when he'd finished, proudly holding the paddles above his head.

'Not bad, I suppose, for you.'

'Not bad?' Dorcan dropped his arms. He let go the paddles, knelt down, picked up a pebble and tossed it at Sabrax. Sabrax ducked, the pebble sailed over his head, and clattered against the trunk of a tree.

'Stop messing about. Give me a hand here or we'll never get this raft built.'

The brothers worked well together. An hour later, their raft was complete. It was four Clyke lengths long by two Clyke lengths wide.

'It looks as if it'll carry us across, doesn't it?' said Sabrax.

'Yes it does. It really does.'

'Well, it should be proof against most things. Let's go.'

Dorcan put the paddles on board the boat as Sabrax

loaded their bags and lines. The pair dragged the craft the short distance to the water's edge. They attempted to launch it, but the front end remained stubbornly grounded in the gravel.

'We'll have to give it a good old heave-ho,' said Sabrax.

Going around to the back of the raft, the two Clykes took hold and shoved with all their might. Gradually the front of the raft moved forward onto the water and finally began to float. Sabrax and Dorcan clambered aboard and, picking up a paddle each, took up positions on either side of the raft.

'Ready?' said Sabrax.

'All set.'

Pulling on their paddles, the two Clykes steered the raft through the reeds and out into open water. Then they began to build a rhythm, the paddles going in, out, in, out, the raft moving faster and faster.

'Hey, look at us, on our own raft,' said Dorcan, turning to Sabrax and smiling. He started whistling.

The raft floated well in the water. Sabrax looked over his shoulder, back towards the shore.

'I reckon if we keep this up, we'll make the other side well before nightfall.'

This was what Dorcan wanted to hear.

Below the surface of the lake a huge pike lurked. The fish had split fins and scarred scales and was ten times the size of the raft. Drawn by the vibrations made by the brothers' splashing, the predator had found the source and now stood off, fins wafting to and fro, content just to follow and wait, watching the small paddles as they beat the water.

After an hour and a half of concerted paddling, Sabrax and Dorcan had reached the middle of the lake. They paused for a moment and gazed around at the great expanse of water. The bright day was gone now, the sky filled with threatening grey clouds. They carried on paddling. A slight breeze got up and it wasn't long before the calm surface of the lake turned to shallow ripples. The breeze stiffened, blowing the ripples together until they rose up as small waves. These small waves lapped against the Clykes' raft, rocking it from side to side. As the breeze turned to a light wind, so the small waves grew bigger. Now they broke as spray over the front of the raft.

'I'm scared.'

'Just keep paddling,' said Sabrax, 'we can do it.'

The two Clykes pulled harder on their paddles, the lake water swilling over the raft. Then a freak wave reared up and slammed against the side of the raft, sweeping Dorcan overboard.

'Help! Sabrax. Help me,' he shrieked, treading water amid the waves, arms flailing as he struggled to stay afloat.

Through the swirling water, the great pike saw Dorcan's legs as they thrashed about. It darted forward.

Without hesitating, Sabrax reached down into the surging water and seized his brother's hands. He hauled him back on board. A wave parted like a curtain; the pike's head appeared. The two Clykes stared at the cruel eyes, cavernous mouth and sharp needle teeth. The pike snapped its mouth shut in a sickening crunch on the end of the raft, sending it backwards. Sabrax fell over heavily. Both paddles slid into the lake.

'Sabrax!'

'Quiet.'

'I'm frightened.'

'Qui-et,' hissed Sabrax.

'Sorry. Can you see it?'

'No. No, I can't. It must have swum away.'

Spray spiralled from the front of the raft, soaking them.

'We've lost our paddles,' whispered Dorcan.

'I know we have.'

'What are we going to do?'

'Nothing. There's nothing we can do. Take out your axe.'

'What for?'

'Just do it. And do what I do.'

Sabrax got out his axe and drove the spiked end into the deck. He tied his line to the handle and then around his waist.

'It'll stop us being swept overboard.'

Dorcan did the same.

All the brothers' efforts had been to no avail. Sabrax gazed at the tall trees of Mailcann forest, the wind and waves carrying them further and further away, driving the raft, rising and falling, back to the shore. The two Clykes sat in silence, wondering if the fish would attack again. Waves buffeted the craft, threatening to smash it. Every now and then a wave would roll right under the raft, causing it to rear up. They knew that, should a wave turn them over, they were doomed. If they did not drown, the fish might well be there to devour them. Suddenly the raft was knocked sideways.

'It's the fish,' yelled Dorcan, a note of terror in his voice, 'there, look.'

Dorcan pointed to the top of the pike's head showing above the waves. The pike butted the raft again.

'It's taunting us, playing with us,' Sabrax whispered, 'it hasn't given up.'

The two Clykes rode uneasily on the raft, expecting an attack at any time.

An hour later, the raft reached the shallows and became entangled in the reeds. Now it was at the mercy of the battering waves. Sabrax glanced at Dorcan, who was clearly terrified. He put his arm around him.

'We must get off.'

Dorcan nodded. Sabrax wrenched his axe from the deck, stowed it in his bag and coiled his line, Dorcan struggling to do the same. The two Clykes got unsteadily to their feet, the raft still tilting and butting in the wave-swell. They pulled their bags and lines over their shoulders. Sabrax crouched down.

'We'll go after the next wave,' said Sabrax, 'ready?'

'Ready.'

The raft was lifted up by a shorebound wave and dropped.

'Now.'

Sabrax sprang from the raft into the lake. Dorcan leapt after him. Carrying their belongings above their heads, the brothers waded chest high as fast as they could through the water towards the beach.

'Come on. Come on,' urged Sabrax.

Dorcan glanced over his shoulder.

'The fish,' he cried despairingly.

The two Clykes struggled to stay upright, forging

forward through the water, away from the pike that had followed them in. More waves raised by the wind swilled about, buffeting the brothers' legs, threatening to overwhelm them. The swirling water hissed and tugged. Then a great wave washed over them both, knocking them flat. They struggled to their feet.

'No-o-o-o-o-o-o,' shouted Dorcan. The pike was upon him, mouth open in readiness to seize him. Dorcan stared at the skewering teeth.

'Don't let it get you,' screamed Sabrax.

Dorcan stood spellbound as the pike thrashed about, its jaws opening and snapping shut only inches from his face. Sabrax waded through the waves and dragged his brother away, backing off from the massive fish. The pike had run out of water. It was stranded on the gravel.

'Blood and sand,' gasped Sabrax, 'look at the size of it.'

'A monster. Under our raft as we've paddled. Whose idea was it to build a raft?'

*

Chapter Eight

The wind had lessened and the squall had passed. Dorcan and Sabrax sat on a slope under a tree, gazing out over the lake. The huge pike lay dead on its side in the shallows, mouth agape, its jaws set in a final snap. Their abandoned raft bobbed in the swell, being first drawn out then brought back in. Spinning in the troughs between the crests, the lost paddles rose and fell with each shore-bound wave. A loud horn blared. Sabrax and Dorcan got hurriedly to their feet and ran back into cover.

'What is it?'

'No idea,' said Sabrax.

Sabrax parted the grasses and peered out. He scanned the lake and at first did not see the prow of the massive ship as it emerged from behind a headland. The horn blew again.

'Wait till you see this,' said Sabrax.

Dorcan rushed to him.

'Oh my goodness. A ship - it's a Tallun ship. Just look

at it.'

The huge lake ferry cleared the headland and slid towards them through the water.

'Fan-tastic,' said Sabrax excitedly, 'and see, there's a red and white flag like ours flying at the stern.'

The two Clykes watched the ferry approach and glide by. They saw Talluns sitting behind windows on the lower decks. On the upper open deck, more Talluns strolled about. A group of Tallun musicians was plucking and blowing on shiny instruments, their music drifting out over the water. After the ferry had passed, they heard the dull rumble of its engines. Soon, the ferry was lost behind another headland.

'What did you make of that?'

'Some of those Talluns must be very clever, to build something like that,' said Dorcan, 'all we can manage are simple wooden rafts.'

It was then that the brothers noticed the great wave that had risen up in the ferry's wake.

'What a wave,' Sabrax cried, his eyes wide, 'and it's building all the time.'

The monster wave ran at an angle towards the place where the Clykes stood. By now it was ten Clykes high, the roar from its tumbling crest growing louder and louder as it ran to shore. The wave arrived, crashing and spreading out in a sweeping wash that gathered up the dead pike, rushing it further up the beach. The wash subsided and leaked away through the gravels, leaving the dead pike stranded again. Sabrax and Dorcan looked at each other.

'We'd still be out on the lake on the raft, if the pike hadn't attacked us,' said Sabrax slowly, 'we'd have been caught and overthrown by that wave. I don't think either of us would have survived.'

'Now what?'

'We'll have to walk round, I suppose,' said Sabrax.

The brothers picked up their bags and lines and headed off into the grasses. The fields in which the two Clykes walked were bounded on three sides by either walls or hedges, but open to the lakeshore. Here they had been made stock proof with barbed wire fences. Huge oak and beech trees grew in the fields. Under their outstretched branches, sheep lay dozing. As they travelled, the brothers continued their usual conversations and speculations: whether there was a certain type of lightning that ripened the corn, what colour was a winter wind, or how many Clykes it would take to build a Tallun ship. They could hear a great noise of traffic and saw vehicles flashing past through gaps in some of the neglected hedges.

Going under the bottom bar of a gate set in a wall, the brothers emerged in a vast area coated in tarmac. Many vehicles, all apparently empty, stood around this area.

'Looks all clear to cross,' began Dorcan.

A dog locked in one of the vehicles saw the Clykes. It began to bark frantically. It rocked the car in its excitement. Orange lights flashed. Waw waw, waw waw, went the car alarm, the car park suddenly filling with noise. Dorcan and Sabrax scuttled back under the gate.

'Can't go any further. Can't run the risk of being seen.'

'No luck,' said Dorcan, 'what do we do now?'

'We'll have to go back and walk the other way round

the lake.'

'That'll take forever.'

'We've no choice.'

'Yes you have,' said a voice.

Sabrax and Dorcan looked up. A crow perched high above them on the branch of an oak tree.

'Is there another way to get across?' asked Sabrax.

'Yes,' said the crow, 'follow me.'

The bird slipped from the oak. It flew to another tree not far away that stood by a tangle of rhododendrons near the shore. The two Clykes moved warily through the short grasses, following the crow.

'Do you think it's a trap?' asked Dorcan.

'Dunno, but we'll soon find out.'

Sabrax and Dorcan walked out of the grasses beneath the rowan in which the crow now perched.

'All you have to do is blow this whistle,' said the crow, pointing with the tip of a wing to a silver whistle hanging on a branch, 'it'll get you across.'

The bird folded its wings.

'How?' asked Sabrax.

'It will. You'll see.'

Sabrax put his bag down and started to climb up the trunk. He'd only got as far as the first branch when a deep, gruff voice called out to him from the middle of the rhododendrons.

'What do you think you're doing?'

The rhododendron leaves rustled and shook. A huge ferret emerged. Sabrax stared at the ferret's sharp claws and a muzzle that bore the scars of many battles.

'That whistle belongs to me.'

Sabrax dropped to the ground. The creature rose up on

its haunches to tower over him.

'The crow said it would get us across the water,' explained Sabrax, stepping backwards.

He put a hand to his mustard pouch and looked up into the ferret's eyes.

'He's right, it will, if you blow it, and you can only blow it if you can take it - from me.'

'You want me to fight you?'

'You'll have to, if you want to get across.'

Sabrax walked over to Dorcan.

'We'll stroll around the lake, it's a pleasant evening.'

'Stand over there by the wall,' said Sabrax, 'if anything happens to me, go and get help to retrieve the you-know-what.'

'You're going to fight it on your own? Can't I fight alongside? Two of us would have more of a chance.'

'I've got to do this by myself, my brave little brother. No use us both ending up as ferret food.'

'Of course, you're right. I see what you mean.'

Sabrax slid the cover off his tree axe and gripped the shaft with both hands. He swung the axe through the air, the head whistling and tharrumming as the sunlight glinted on its honed edge. Sabrax stopped suddenly and raised the axe high above his head. He grinned at Dorcan.

'Clykes away!'

'Clykes away! You can do it, Sabs.'

Sabrax walked forward. The ferret moved to and fro excitedly in front of him.

'I'm ready.' Sabrax gripped his axe tightly.

'To die?' said the ferret, running a paw through its whiskers, 'come along, my little friend,' it growled, 'come to my jaws. I'll crunch you in two and chew and swallow you.'

Sabrax held his axe out in his right hand and showed its razor sharp edge to the creature.

'Look on my axe and tremble, Ferret, for it will be the death of you.'

Sabrax and the ferret circled each other, their eyes locked, each waiting for the other to make a move. Without warning, the ferret lunged forward, jagged teeth ripping Sabrax's shirt. A trickle of blood ran down Sabrax's chest.

'I smell blood,' said the ferret.

The ferret pounced again, but Sabrax anticipated the move, stepped aside, swung his axe and cut several whiskers from the animal's face. The ferret drew back smartly. Sabrax rushed it, shrieking. Unnerved, the ferret blinked. Sabrax swung his axe, the head bit deep into a paw. The wounded animal struck out, bowling Sabrax over. He sprang up as the ferret attacked again, its jaws snapping in front of his face. Leaping out of the way, Sabrax landed awkwardly, turned an ankle and fell to the ground. He dropped his axe.

'No,' shouted Dorcan.

He turned away and could not look as the ferret fell upon his brother, pinning him to the ground with its paws. Sabrax gazed up at the widening jaws as the ferret drew its head back and made ready to savage him. He felt for his axe, seized the handle and, with one final effort, swung it. The axe struck point first between an eye and an ear on the ferret's head. For several seconds the animal froze, staring at Sabrax in disbelief. Slowly it slipped sideways to the ground. Dorcan ran across from the edge of the clearing to where Sabrax lay.

'You've killed it,' he said, lifting the ferret's paws from his brother's chest, 'my goodness, you've beaten a ferret. Just wait till they hear all about this at home. Oh my.'

Drained by his efforts, Sabrax rolled over and lay face down on the ground, trembling.

'Are you all right?'

'It's nothing,' said Sabrax, 'I'm fine.'

'Well done,' said the crow.

'This is Sabrax Clyke,' said Dorcan, 'he doesn't stand any nonsense from ferrets.'

The crow nodded. 'So I see.'

Getting to his feet, Sabrax staggered about, beating the dust from his clothes. Dorcan shinned up the tree and lifted the whistle from the branch. Turning the whistle upside down, he shook it. A spider fell out.

'Off you go, off you go.'

Sabrax retrieved his axe from the dead ferret's head. He wiped the blood from the axe on the animal's fur. Dorcan scrambled down from the tree.

'Look,' said Dorcan, pointing to a series of incised letters on the whistle, 'there are Tallun signs on it.'

Sabrax took the whistle off him and studied it.

'I wonder what they say?'

'My single note will bring, one to carry you, whistling,' said the crow.

'How do you know that?' asked Dorcan, looking bemused.

'That's for me to know, and for you to find out. You'll have to blow it - if you still intend to cross the lake, that is.'

Sabrax polished the whistle with his shirt cuff. He

moistened his lips, put the whistle to his mouth and blew it.

Peeeeeeeeeeeeeeeeeeeep.

The single note echoed over the water. The two Clykes stared out, unsure what it was they were looking for.

'Try again,' said the crow.

Sabrax raised the whistle to his lips. He blew a longer note this time.

Peeeeeeeeeeeeeeeeeeeeeeeeeeeeeeeeeeeeeeeeeeep.

The brothers stared out over the water again.

'There,' said Sabrax, pointing.

In the distance, on the far side of the lake, they saw a great white bird rise up. It ran across the water beating its wings and was soon airborne. In no time at all it had crossed the lake. It bore down on the brothers.

'Listen,' said Dorcan, 'whistling wings.'

'One to carry you, whistling,' said the crow.

'What is it?' asked Dorcan.

'A bird,' replied Sabrax.

'I know that much, what *kind* of bird is it?'

'A swan.'

'Well, well, well,' he said, looking at Sabrax and smiling, 'it's a swan. A real, live swan.'

'Now I must leave you,' said the crow, 'goodbye, and good luck. I think you may well need it.'

Dropping out of the tree, it flew lazily away.

The swan glided down, skimming the surface of the lake. Webbed feet thrust out, it pushed against the water, its body creating a bow wave until it came to rest. The swan folded its wings, shook its head and long neck and coasted towards them.

'What do we do now?' said Dorcan.

Sabrax put the whistle in his bag as the big bird stepped out of the shallows.

'Should we climb aboard, Swan?' asked Sabrax.

'Sssssssss,' hissed the swan.

'I think that's a "yes".'

Sabrax and Dorcan tossed their bags and lines onto the swan's back. Taking hold of the bird's large body feathers, the brothers scrambled up and got to their feet.

'We're ready, Swan,' said Sabrax.

Bowing its head, the swan stood up, turned around, walked back into the water and this time set off paddling back across the lake, its powerful webbed feet propelling it forward. Soon the shore was left far behind.

'Its quite straightforward, sailing on a swan,' said Dorcan confidently, leaning back on the bird's neck. He slipped sideways, Sabrax seizing hold of him, only his lightning quick reactions between his brother and a dip in the lake.

'Yes it is,' said Sabrax, 'quite straightforward.'

Dorcan ignored him and straightened his coat.

The swan paddled steadily out into the lake, all the while Sabrax and Dorcan talking excitedly and pointing to features and hills. Soon they had passed the halfway point, the far shore and huge trees of Mailcann Forest fast approaching. The brothers stopped chattering. They gazed in silence at the stands of trees, then glanced at each other, neither face betraying their inner anxieties. The most dangerous part of their journey was almost upon them, and they knew they would soon be tested.

When the swan reached the shore, it waded out of the water, walked up the beach and squatted.

'Come on,' urged Sabrax.

He threw off his bag and line and leapt down after them. Dorcan lost his foothold, slithered over the feathers and tumbled down. He ended up in a heap on the shore with his bag and climbing line piled on top of him. He got to his feet, brushed off his clothes and straightened his coat. The swan turned its long neck, lowered its head and had a good look at this small clumsy creature.

'Your feathers are too slippy,' said Dorcan.

The swan bent its head towards Sabrax and let him stroke its beak. Then the bird walked down to the water, paddled out and glided away.

Dorcan and Sabrax left their bags and lines on the shore. They strode up the beach right to the edge of the forest.

'I feel even smaller here,' said Dorcan, staring at the stands of giant pine trees rising up into the sky.

Huge pinecones dotted the ground. There were no bright flowers or plants to be seen, just masses of pine needles forming a monotonous, level surface that stretched away and was lost in the darkness under the trees.

'What do you think?'

'It's a strange place, all right,' said Sabrax.

'I don't like the look of it.'

'Let's go and get our things.'

Sabrax and Dorcan turned and headed back down the beach. As they walked, Sabrax glanced at Dorcan. He saw the worried look on his brother's face.

'Come on. Cheer up. We've got this far against all the odds.'

'Yes, but this is the worst bit, isn't it, said Dorcan, 'just wondering if we'd be safer sleeping here on the shore tonight? Go into the forest first thing in the morning.'

*

Chapter Nine

Long Hall had been decorated with colourful streamers and purple bunting for Calamorica's birthnight, and now a noisy party was under way. Each Clyke was wearing the hat they'd made during the day and that evening a prize would be awarded for the most original. Calamorica sat at the big dining table surrounded by birthnight presents. She wore her best clothes and the fine pair of new green boots that Woadica had made for her. Durabito sat beside Calamorica. They were deep in conversation. Cataporinganio came over to join them.

'Where are Sabrax and Dorcan? Not coming?'

'It is unfortunate,' said Calamorica, shaking her head slowly, 'but they're away. Looking for something, er, that's not really lost, more mislaid.'

'What kind of thing,' asked Cataporinganio, turning to face them both, 'mmm?'

'What was it again, Durabito?'

'Er, it's a staff. Sabrax made it. For Calamorica. For her birthnight.'

'Yes, that's it, a staff,' said Calamorica, nodding.

'I thought birthnight presents were supposed to be a surprise?' said Cataporinganio, frowning.

'I dropped a hint to Sabrax that I'd like one.'

'You'd always wanted one, hadn't you?' said Durabito.

'Yes.'

'It takes two to find a staff?'

'Sabrax wasn't sure on which side of the wall it had been mislaid. He's walking on one side, Dorcan's walking on the other. Aren't they?'

'They are, Calamorica,' said Durabito, 'they are.'

A great cheer rose up in the Hall as Longalio came in carrying the birthnight cake. Calamorica and Durabito looked at each other.

'Saved by the cake,' whispered Calamorica.

Twenty bright green candles, one for every ten summers, dotted the top of the birthnight cake, everyone applauding it. Calamorica dabbed her glistening eyes with a large, red and white spotted handkerchief.

'For me?'

'For you,' said Longalio, setting the cake down on the table in front of her.

Longalio got a burning twig from the fire and lit the candles. The Clykes began to chant.

'Blow them out, blow them out.'

Calamorica stood up. She rested her hands on the edge of the table, leaned over the cake, drew in a breath and blew with all her might.

'Phwoooooooooooooooor.'

Twenty candles were extinguished in one puff. All the Clykes present made a silent wish.

'The cake, the cake, cut the cake,' shouted the Clykes.

Calamorica picked up a knife from the table and cut a slice of birthnight cake as the Clykes cheered and sang a song of happy birthnights to come. Longalio cut up the rest of the cake and everyone there was given a piece. He put two pieces aside for Sabrax and Dorcan.

Later, when the party had finally subsided and tired Clykes had gone to bed, Cataporinganio and Calamorica sat together talking by the fire in Long Hall.

'You'd tell me if there was a problem,' he said, 'let me help?'

'Oh, of course I would. Certainly I would.'

'Only I have the distinct feeling there's something not quite right.'

'Oh, no, there's nothing amiss here. Anyway, how could I possibly conceal anything from you?'

'You wouldn't try to, would you?'

'Me? Attempt to deceive a wizard? Not likely.'

*

Dorcan had made a crude shelter out of several big stones, a few thick briar stems and some large leaves. He was making final adjustments to the roof.

'Take his mind off it all,' muttered Sabrax, watching him, 'he's happiest when he's busy.'

Then Dorcan got down on his knees. He crawled into his shelter, set out his sleeping sack, wriggled into it, made himself comfortable and gave a deep, contented sigh.

'Night, Sabrax. We'll be all right here, won't we?'

'Of course we will. Goodnight, Dorcs, sleep well.'

More sighs and grunts came from the shelter as Dorcan

settled. Loud snores finally indicated that he had fallen asleep. Sabrax took cover under a clump of thick grass. He sat upright in his sleeping sack and hummed an old Clyke tune. He gazed at the stars ranged in the black night sky. A star fell; Sabrax saw it and made a wish.

'A safe day tomorrow.'

He wriggled down into his sleeping sack and laid his head on the pillow of boots and line. He closed his eyes and thought about tall grasses waving and swishing in the breeze in summer haymeadows at home. He drifted slowly into sleep.

*

'Well, I must be off,' said Cataporinganio, gazing out to the hills in the distance, black in the dawn light, 'got to get back to my mountains. Looks like it's going to be a fine day. Been delightful being among you all again. I've enjoyed every minute. Will you watch me go?'

'Of course I will,' said Calamorica, 'I can't tell you how pleased I was that you journeyed here to celebrate my birthnight, and that it was such a, er, success. Come along now, let's get you safely away.'

The two old friends put their arms around each other and strolled out of the wall.

'I expect it will be a while before we see you again,' said Calamorica, when they reached a clearing.

'Who knows?'

Cataporinganio pressed her hand. He walked to the middle of the clearing and turned to face her.

'Goodbye, dear Calamorica.'

'Goodbye, old friend.'

In one swift movement, Cataporinganio seized the hem of his cape and pulled it over his head. There was a bright flash of light and when Calamorica looked again, she saw he had retaken the form of a raven. The raven sprang into the air and vanished into the dawn on powerful beating wings. Calamorica stood and mopped her sweating brow with her handkerchief.

'What an ordeal,' she muttered. 'I think we managed to fool him, though.'

*

Sabrax woke early. His attention was drawn to the cries of young starlings that had roosted in the tall trees nearby and now winged in great flocks across the dawn sky. He gazed up at the mass of birds. A sudden loud snore drew his gaze sideways to Dorcan's shelter.

'Sleep on hot embers,' he muttered.

He picked up a handful of small pebbles, and taking careful aim, cast the pebbles one by one onto the roof of the shelter. The pebbles accumulated in a slight hollow before sliding with a rush inside.

'What the . . . it's raining stones,' shouted Dorcan, scrambling out of his shelter. He stood up hurriedly. 'You,' he bellowed, pointing to Sabrax, 'how could you do that to a little Clyke like me? I might have fainted or something. Then you'd be sorry.'

'Come on, lazy legs. We've an appointment with a hawk.'

After they had washed in the lake and put on fresh clothes, the brothers gathered up their belongings and stowed them in their bags.

Sabrax saw that Dorcan was subdued. He put his arm around his shoulder.

'I know you're worried.'

'Worried? Petrified more like.'

'Don't be. It'll be all right.'

'Huge hungry hawk with sharp talons.'

'I swear to you that we'll succeed.'

'It won't get us?'

'No. I'll take good care of you.'

'Promise?'

'I promise,' said Sabrax.

'What are we waiting for? Let's go.'

The two Clykes picked up their bags, slung their climbing lines over their shoulders and made their way up the beach to the edge of the forest.

'Which way?' asked Dorcan, staring at the forest's dark interior.

'Straight ahead, according to the swallows.'

Sabrax walked off and Dorcan followed. There were no discernible paths or tracks to follow, Sabrax marking the route they were taking by cutting arrows in tree roots with his axe, pointing back to the beach. Finding their way out of the forest would be simple.

The further the brothers ventured into the depths of the forest, the darker it became.

'Look at those branches,' said Sabrax, pointing to the dense canopy overhead, 'all grown together - shutting out the daylight.'

'Like walking at night. Should have brought candles. Whooaaaowww!' Dorcan sank up to his hips in a hidden hollow beneath the carpet of pine needles. 'Blast it. Blast it, and treble blast it.'

Dorcan wriggled and struggled in an attempt to extricate himself, but this only made things worse, for he slipped down deeper into the mass of needles. Sabrax took hold of his brother's hands, spread his stance and pulled him up and out of the hollow in one swift movement.

'Heavy going this,' said Dorcan, shaking pine needles from his clothes and boots.

'Never mind, just concentrate on the task in hand and try to watch where you're placing your feet.'

Keek, Keek, Keek, Keek, Keekeekkkeee.

Krokr Longtoe's chilling cry echoed through the forest.

Dorcan and Sabrax looked at each other.

'Sabrax?'

Keek, Keek, Keek, Keek, Keekeekkkeee.

'D'you think it's seen us?' said Dorcan nervously.

'It might have. I don't know.'

'Where is it?' he whispered.

'No idea, but I have a feeling we'll soon find out. Let's keep going.'

The brothers walked warily now, gazing up at the branches, trying to catch a glimpse of the hawk. Dry pine needles snapping underfoot betrayed their presence with every step.

'There, look.'

Sabrax pointed to a giant pine tree standing illuminated in a circle of daylight amid the forest's gloom. Its width was that of three ordinary trees.

'Come on,' said Sabrax. He strode off towards it.

'Wait.' Dorcan hurried after him.

Sabrax reached the tree first, patting the rough bark as he gazed up through the maze of branches.

'There's a nest. Look, up there,' he said, pointing to a mass of twigs at the very top of the tree, silhouetted against the sky. 'This must be it.'

'What good news.'

'Cheer up.'

'Well, it doesn't seem to bother you, all this. Chasing hawks and everything.'

'Have faith in your ability,' said Sabrax, 'you're a tough Clyke. I've always thought that.'

'Have you? Really?'

'Of course.'

'Oh.'

'Hey, look at this.' Sabrax went across to an old tree stump nearby.

He and Dorcan walked among the bird skulls, piles of feathers and old animal bones strewn over the ground.

'Remains of hawk prey,' whispered Dorcan, anxious in case the hawk should hear him, 'it's a plucking post. Seen them before. It's where the hawk strips the feathers or fur off what it's caught, before it carries it to the nest. Great badger beards . . . what am I saying. That could be us.'

'If we're not vigilant.'

Sabrax searched among the bones and feathers. He kicked them over with his boots.

'What are you looking for?' whispered Dorcan.

'Nothing in particular. Just seeing what's here. Listen.' Sabrax pointed into the forest.

'Can't hear . . . '

'There.'

A flock of swallows appeared out of the trees and flew at full speed towards the two Clykes.

'This is it. This is it,' the birds twittered, circling the pine.

'Well done, swallows. Thank you for your help,' Sabrax called to them. 'Now you must get away, all of you. You've done well. Go to safety now.'

Twittering loudly, the swallows flew away.

'This is the tree, Dorcan.'

'Oh dear. I feel ill.'

*

Chapter Ten

It was midday. Calamorica and Longalio sat together in the shadow of the wall, keeping watch over the baby Clykes playing at their feet. The rest of the Clykes were scattered throughout the wall, most of them asleep, as it was far too hot for working. Some had chosen shade, while others lay out in the sun on the camstones on top of the wall.

'What a party,' said Longalio.

He took a sip of cowslip cordial.

'It was.'

'I thought you rallied very well.'

'Yes, I did,' said Calamorica, nodding her head slowly in agreement with his observation, 'least I could do.'

'We all wanted you to enjoy Cataporinganio's visit.'

'I did enjoy it. It was the topping on the cake really, him coming to see me.'

'Yes. That's it. The cake. Topping on the cake.'

'What on earth are you mumbling on about?'

'Do you think your excuse as to why Sabrax and

Dorcan were not there really convinced him?' said Longalio, moving on quickly.

'Of course,' replied Calamorica, gazing up at the Clykes asleep on the wall top. 'Just listen to 'em snoring away. Lazy lot. Never saw it in our day, hey? Everyone asleep. No one on guard. What if something should happen?'

'It's the way of it today. They seem to please themselves. We were brought up differently.'

The two Clykes sat and hurh-hurged under their breath as they stared out at the glare of the afternoon. The little Clykes rolled around their feet in the dust. Some of the other youngsters had climbed up into the bushes and now sat with the baby blackbirds in their nest.

'This new fellar next field needs taking in hand,' said Calamorica, 'his walls are in a poor state and his hen huts - it doesn't bear thinking about. They need fettling, no doubt about it, fettling. What's missing, of course, is a Clyke family to look after it. I've sent a message to Borengapor, to see if he's interested. He'd soon knock the new fellar into shape.'

'Borengapor, yes, he'd certainly be up to the job and I know he's looking for a new farm, but do you think it's wise?'

'We must be prepared to forget the past and look forward.'

'Well, in that case,' said Longalio, 'I don't suppose there could be any harm in it.'

'I think it's a rather inspired choice myself.'

A Clyke asleep in the wall put up his hand and brushed something long and whiskery from his face. Another Clyke, prodded by a moist black nose, turned over as he slept.

'Mmmm,' said the stoat, 'lovely plump Clykes. Spoilt for choice. Must have a look at the rest of them.'

A third Clyke woke up in time to see the sleek creature with its dark head, black nose, bright button eyes and long whiskers, slither out of sight among the stones.

'Stoat, stoat, watch out, stoat,' screeched the little owl, from his perch in the tree.

In an instant, the Clykes had scattered from the wall.

'What? A stoat? Blast it. That's all we need,' said Calamorica, getting quickly to her feet, 'where on earth did that come from?'

Longalio hastily gathered up the baby Clykes and took them into the safety of the long grass.

The Clykes milled about on the ground below and bumped into each other in panic and confusion.

'Stoat! Stoat! Hoah! Hoah!'

Clykes ran to Calamorica from all directions, Rosmanda and Durabito among them.

'Right everybody. Calm down. Come along, calm down now.'

The Clykes calmed down.

'Thank you. There's a killer in our wall, a stoat. You have all been trained to deal with these predators and know what you have to do. And take care, all of you.'

Rosmanda stepped forward.

'I'll go into the trap.'

'No, Ros,' said Calamorica, 'it's too dangerous.'

'Who was it got the adder out of the log store?'

'Er, it was you, as I remember,' said Durabito.

'And chased the mink from the riverbank?'

'You,' said Durabito.

'All right,' said Calamorica, 'if you are determined.'

Rosmanda checked her mustard pouch, grabbed her axe and crept into the wall through a nearby hole.

'Come along,' said Calamorica, 'let's go. We've got to get rid of this blasted stoat.'

The rest of the Clykes followed Calamorica into the wall.

The Clykes began their search for the creature by looking in all the rooms that surrounded Long Hall. There was no sign of it.

'See anything?' whispered Calamorica.

'Nothing,' replied Durabito, 'but it's in here somewhere. I can smell it.'

'We'll start a forward sweep,' said Calamorica, giving a stone three sharp taps with the end of her staff. It was the signal for the rest of the Clykes to move.

Everyone began to shout loudly and bang their staffs on the stones. Rosmanda had reached the trap and now stood on a small gallery that ran at high level around the walls. She could hear the rest shouting to each other and rattling on the stones with their staffs as they made their way steadily towards her. Suddenly the stoat rushed into the trap, saw Rosmanda on the gallery, leapt up and attacked her. She stepped backwards smartly as the enraged creature bit its way clean through the handrail in a frenzied attempt to seize her. She grabbed a handful of mustard from her pouch and cast it in the stoat's face. Stung and blinded by the mustard, the creature lashed out and pulled down a whole section of gallery with a rake of its paws. Rosmanda sprang onto the creature's back, seized hold of a tuft of its fur and hung on.

'Want to kill me do you?' she shouted at the snarling animal, as it tried to sink its teeth into her.

She raised her axe. The stoat swung round and tossed her from its back. She tumbled heavily. Her axe flew from her grip, clattering loudly as it slid away. She lay winded on the floor. Somehow she managed to stagger to her feet but the stoat seized her with its paws and pinned her up against the wall. Rosmanda stared at the creature's glistening fangs.

'Ooo. What a lovely plump Clyke,' said the stoat.

Suddenly a party of Clykes appeared in the trap. They beat the stoat with their staffs. The stoat turned its attention from Rosmanda and attacked them fiercely. Reinforcements arrived and soon the stoat had dozens more staffs drumming on its head. The Clykes drove the stoat back, all the time the creature snapping and spitting at them.

'Out! Out! Out!'

More and more Clykes piled into the trap. Now it seemed as if a great spiny animal attacked the stoat, so many were the staffs. Pulling on ropes, the Clykes hoisted up the wide slate that covered a passage from the wall and drove the stoat out. The ropes were let go; the slate dropped back down with a thud, sealing the chamber. Clykes ran to spy holes. They watched the defeated killer lurch off into the grass, still sneezing violently.

'Goodbye, Stoat,' shouted Rosmanda, retrieving her axe, 'you won't be eating a Clyke today.'

Longalio carried the little Clykes out of the meadow grasses. The young Clykes that had remained hidden in the blackbird's nest climbed down as the parent blackbirds flew across to their young. All the Clykes gathered together in the lee of the wall.

'Are you all right, Rosmanda?' asked Calamorica.

'I'm fine.'

'Anyone hurt? No? Good. It'll think twice before it bothers us again,' said Calamorica. She shook her fist. 'Marvellous, brave Clykes. Rosmanda, all of you, and that includes the younger ones. So brave.'

Clykes cheered and raised their hands above their heads in a victory salute.

'Well, they might be lazy,' began Longalio.

'But they're every bit as brave as we were,' concluded Calamorica.

*

Dorcan and Sabrax's climbing equipment was laid out on the ground in front of them, the brothers looking pensive as they pulled on their spiked boots. They tied their twine bootlaces tight. Sabrax stood up

'Right,' said Sabrax, 'let's get this over with. Soon be on our way home.'

'You reckon?'

'I do. My promise, remember?'

Sabrax slid his arm around his brother's shoulders and hugged him. He rolled up his shirtsleeves and tied the first length of line round his waist. He moved across to the giant pine.

'Safe climb, Sabrax.'

'You too, Dorcan. Good luck.'

Sabrax looked up and studied a possible route. He checked his line, dug his boot spikes in and took a firm grip of the rough bark. He began to climb and it wasn't long before he'd got a rhythm going, digging in with his spikes and pulling up with his hands. Dorcan let the line run out as he watched his brother attack the tree. Sabrax climbed up and up and up, moving swiftly between the branches. Dorcan paid out and knotted, line to line.

'What's it like?' Dorcan shouted up.

'Not bad.'

There were plenty of good, firm handholds and when Sabrax kicked in his spikes, they bit deep into the bark. He neither paused nor looked back, but moved steadily on up the pine. Soon he was sitting astride a branch about halfway up the tree. After he had secured his line, he waved his arm and gestured for Dorcan to follow him up. Dorcan tied the line around his waist and started to climb. Both were powerful, nimble climbers, the best of all the Clykes. Sabrax drew in the slack on Dorcan's line, watching as he made steady progress up the tree. There was deftness to Dorcan's climbing, thought Sabrax, his brother gripping the bark, stretching his legs and digging in his spikes firmly. Dorcan reached the branch where Sabrax waited.

'You're a good climber.'

'I know.'

'Long way up,' teased Sabrax.

'Long way down.' Dorcan stared at the forest floor.

'Halfway. Let's keep going.'

Sabrax began to climb again and soon got back into his rhythm, advancing quickly and confidently over the bark, seeking out handholds. Dorcan watched him go, making sure the line did not snag on anything. Sabrax fairly raced up the tree and was soon tied on again, this time to a branch near the very top, just below the nest. He looked at the mass of twigs above his head. Then he waved for Dorcan to climb up. In no time at all, Dorcan appeared at Sabrax's feet. He clambered onto the branch and tied on.

'The nest?'

'The nest. One final effort.'

'I daren't look down.' Dorcan looked pale, his legs trembled visibly.

'Just you concentrate on what you're doing. You'll soon forget you're at the top of a tree. Ready?'

'Yes.'

Sabrax untied himself from the branch and began to climb again. Dorcan paid out the line and watched nervously as his brother began to tackle the enormous nest overhang. In a few moves, Sabrax had found a clear route and had climbed halfway up the underside.

'Are you all right?'

'Yes,' said Sabrax.

Holding on tightly with his left hand to a twig rooted firmly in the nest, Sabrax reached with his right hand to another twig above his head. He grabbed hold of it and began to pull himself up. There was a loud crack. The twig snapped. It struck him in the face. The jolt made him lose his footholds, his legs swinging in an arc out into the air, pulling him away from the nest. Now he hung there, his left hand tight around a twig, his body weight supported on one arm, legs dangling.

'Don't fall,' shouted Dorcan, 'oh please, don't fall.'

Sabrax glanced down at the fearsome drop to earth.

'May all my ancestors be with me at this moment and give me strength,' Sabrax whispered in his fear.

Dorcan could not bear to look now. Sheer terror had silenced him. Sabrax appeared to be beaten.

'Come on, come on,' Sabrax muttered, 'don't give in now.'

Slowly Sabrax bent his arm, his body shaking with the effort. He rose up gradually and painfully until he was within grabbing distance of yet another twig in the nest. He seized one with his free hand. The twig held. He hung there.

'Sabrax?'

'I'm fine. Fine.'

Now Sabrax raised his legs and found safe footholds in the nest fabric. He paused for only the briefest of moments to get his breath back, and continued his climb. In five more moves he reached the nest lip. Taking a firm grip, he pulled himself up and over. He got quickly to his feet. He scanned the litter in the nest and began to tear at it with his hands. He cast three long pigeon flight feathers out of his way, along with the remains of a robin. It was as he searched among the bits of prey skin and body feathers, that he discovered the missing bonnet. The precious brooch was still fastened to it.

'Y-e-s-s-s-s,' he shouted, snatching it up.

He unpinned the talisman, wrapped it in his handkerchief and put it safely in his pocket.

'Yeesss,' he said again, pure joy surging through him.

He turned to go and stopped dead. The two large, yellow, taloned feet and long thin legs of Krokr Longtoe obstructed his way back. Sabrax looked up slowly, his eyes moving over the barred body feathers and on up until they settled on the cruel visage, the hooked bill and the fierce yellow eyes. Suddenly Krokr attacked Sabrax with his sharp beak. Sabrax sidestepped the lunge, only for his right leg to sink through the nest platform. He got his trapped leg free of the mass of twigs and swerved to one side again, as Krokr snatched at him with his long middle toe. Krokr struck a third time. Sabrax stumbled trying to avoid the flash of talons, lost his balance and staggered backwards. He fell right out of the nest.

Dorcan saw his brother fall. In an instant he had swung his tree axe and buried its head deep into the tree. As Sabrax hurtled past, Dorcan stamped the spikes of both boots into the bark and braced himself. He waited and waited for his brother to slam to a halt at the end of his line, all the time watching Sabrax as he fell down and down and down.

'Hold axe, please hold,' whispered Dorcan, dwelling on the likelihood of both of them being torn from the tree and sent plunging to their deaths.

'Dunnnnnggggg,' went the line. The axe head held. Dorcan's hands were fast around the axe handle, his whole body straining as he bore his brother's weight, the tight line twanging and vibrating, Sabrax swinging to and fro across the face of the tree.

'Hang on, hang on, while I get a grip,' Sabrax shouted.

Sabrax dug his spikes deep into the bark, seized hold of the tree and clung onto it. The tight line went slack. Dorcan closed his eyes and gasped in relief.

'I've got it. I've got the brooch.'

'Are you all right?'

'I am. I am - and you?'

'Thankful,' said Dorcan, 'er, can we get off this tree now?' He'd already wrenched out his axe and was climbing down to where Sabrax waited for him.

'You've saved my life.'

'Let's get out of here,' muttered Dorcan, 'I've got a

feeling we haven't seen the last of that hawk.'

Sabrax and Dorcan took a quick look up at the hawk's nest. They dug in their spikes and began a mad scramble down the tree. When they reached the bottom, they pulled down their lines and swiftly gathered up their belongings. They speedily retraced their steps out of the forest, following the arrows cut in the tree roots.

Krokr Longtoe had watched the Clykes scurry away. He leapt from his nest and flew off into the dark forest.

Keek, Keek, Keek, Keekeekkkeee.

*

Chapter Eleven

Calamorica stood in front of the hearth in Long Hall. Tears welled up in her eyes and slipped down her cheeks as she contemplated the degree of bad fortune that dogged the Clykes now. Handles had fallen from pails, hammer shafts had broken, butter wouldn't churn, sections of wall had fallen down, bread burned in the ovens and the farm hens had stopped laying.

'Absolute misery, all of it,' she muttered, 'self-inflicted. It's all my fault. Getting old.'

She dabbed her tears with her handkerchief.

'Sabrax and Dorcan, both out risking their lives, all because of me. Wherever you are, take care. If anything were to happen to you . . . it would be too much for me to bear.'

Calamorica picked up a small gold-framed picture from the mantelpiece.

'Cantardio, my dear, what would you make of it all? Our boys trying to make good a mistake I made. Doesn't seem fair, does it?' How I wish I could see you again. You'd know what to do.'

She held the likeness for a moment in her hand, raised it to her lips and kissed it.

*

Dorcan and Sabrax stood on the gravel at the edge of the lake. Sabrax reached into his bag and drew out the whistle.

'Can I blow it this time?' pleaded Dorcan.

Sabrax handed the whistle to him as Dorcan wiped his mouth with the back of his hand in readiness. He put the whistle to his lips and blew it.

Peeeeeeeeeeeeeeeeeeeeeeeeeeeeeeeep.

The swan came at once, the big bird flying directly to the place where the two Clykes stood. It waddled out of the water onto the beach and sat down in front of them.

'Hello, Swan,' said Sabrax, stroking the bird's head, 'thanks for coming so quickly.'

'We're on our way home,' said Dorcan, clambering onto the bird's back, 'so whenever you're ready, Swan.'

'Hey, steady on,' cried Sabrax.

'Are you going to get aboard? Or are we going to wait here all day?'

Sabrax climbed onto the swan's back and put his arm around his brother's shoulder.

'There's no need to get ratty, Dorcan. We'll soon be home. Ready when you are, Swan.'

The swan entered the lake and waddled out until it floated. It paddled off. Dorcan gazed down through the clear water. He saw the swan's powerful legs and webbed feet moving to and fro in a blur, driving it forward, and propelling it at speed. Suddenly the bird unfurled its great wings. Beating the air, it rose up out of the water and ran across the surface of the lake.

'What's it doing?'

'I think it's taking off,' said Sabrax.

'What? You mean it's going to fly?'

'Grab hold of some feathers and don't let go.'

Sabrax and Dorcan hung on to the swan's neck feathers as the bird's powerful wings stroked up and down.

'I'm scared,' shouted Dorcan.

'Too late. Just hang on.'

A loud whistling sound rose up as air streamed over the swan's wings. Sabrax and Dorcan were blasted, their hair dancing on their heads in the turbulence.

As the swan lifted off, the brothers watched the lake fall away beneath them.

'We're flying,' shouted Sabrax over the wind noise.

Five mallard flashed past, the birds quacking loudly. Dorcan was silent and held on grimly to the swan's neck feathers, thinking about the deep water far below.

'There are boats out on the lake,' shouted Sabrax.

Dorcan, hardly daring to move, glanced down.

'See, some of them have got big white sails.'

Clinging on tightly with his hands, Dorcan gestured with nods of his head. 'Out there, look, out there.'

Sabrax turned to look. In the distance, the water of a great sea sparkled and danced in the sunlight. Ahead lay the fields and walls of their home ground, with woods, streams, coppices, farmhouses, roads, fells, ponds and ditches, all spread out in a great pattern.

'Magical,' muttered Sabrax.

The flight did not last long, the swan suddenly holding

its wings out level and starting its long glide down. To Sabrax and Dorcan it now looked as though the lake rushed up to meet them. The bird angled its wings to lessen the airflow and spread out its tail feathers to act as an air brake. With webbed feet splayed, the swan landed on the lake.

'What d'you think about that?'

Dorcan put his hand on his head.

'Is my hair still in place? Or has it been blasted off?'

'Of course it hasn't. Wasn't that fantastic,' said Sabrax excitedly.

'Have you got a comb, Sabrax?'

'Wait until we get back home and tell them we've flown through the air on the back of a swan.'

The swan paddled up to the gravel edge, walked out of the water, up the shingle beach and stopped. Sabrax leapt down from the bird's back.

'Swan, that was incredible. We were flying. Flying through the air.'

The swan bowed its head and hissed softly.

'We couldn't have got across the lake without you. We offer our thanks. Should you ever need help from a Clyke in the future, I can assure you we'll be there.'

The swan wagged its tail and hissed. Dorcan threw down the bags.

'Thanks for the ride, Swan,' he said, jumping down off the bird's back, 'I won't forget that in a hurry.'

Sabrax stroked the swan's head.

'I hope we'll see you again.'

The swan hissed softly. The two Clykes watched the bird turn round, waddle back down the beach and paddle out into the water until it became buoyant. It turned to

114

face the brothers, bowed its head once, then went about and floated away. Sabrax stooped down and rummaged through his bag.

'We'd better put this back,' he said, drawing out the whistle.

'Must we? It'd look good on my bedroom wall at home.'

'Back on the branch it goes. It will be of use to others, no doubt. Anyway, don't tempt fate, we're not home yet.'

Sabrax climbed up the tree, hung the whistle on the branch then scrambled down.

'There's no sign of the ferret,' said Dorcan, 'wonder what's happened to it?'

'Buried by sexton beetles, I expect.'

'Maybe it was eaten by carrion scavengers. Foxes.'

'Or the crow and his friends, perhaps.'

'Nothing surprises me about crows,' said Dorcan.

The brothers picked up their bags and lines and so began the long walk home.

Sabrax, whistling an old Clyke walking tune, strode back up the hill away from the lake. Dorcan trailed along behind him in silence with his head down. It wasn't long before the two Clykes had left the woodland behind and were back among the haymeadows. Sabrax stopped whistling and turned round. Dorcan bumped into him.

'Sorry.'

'Now what are you worrying about?'

'Home. Returning safely.'

'I'll make sure you return safely - I've promised, remember. The worst is over. Now come on, just enjoy the journey.'

Sabrax started whistling again and it wasn't long before Dorcan joined in.

As he strolled along, Sabrax thought about the events of the day, for so much had happened in such a short time. Usually in a Clyke day there were only little occurrences, things that could easily be dealt with and would take no more than a dozen words in the telling. The tale of this journey of theirs would, however, fill many a long winter evening.

'More enjoyable now, the walking, don't you think?' said Dorcan, striding briskly past Sabrax and marching on ahead.

'What? Oh, yes. I know what you mean. Same track we came on, but the journey seems shorter when you're on your way home.'

'That's it exactly. You are good with words, you know.'

'Let's stop for something to eat,' said Sabrax, 'they're more good words aren't they?'

'My favourites.'

Finding shelter from the hot sun under a clump of burdocks, the brothers sat and rested. Sabrax got out a small packet from his bag and unwrapped it. He took out a couple of pieces of pie and began to eat. He soon became aware of being watched. He glanced at Dorcan.

'Where's yours?'

'Eaten it all.'

'You'll never change. What would happen to you if we got lost and still had many nights away from home?'

'I'd probably starve.'

'No you wouldn't, you could live on roots and things.'

'I'd rather starve.'

'Here.' Sabrax handed Dorcan a piece of pie. 'Eat it slowly. Savour it. You won't have any dandelion tea left either?'

'Er, no.'

Sabrax handed his bottle of dandelion tea to Dorcan.

'Thanks, Sabs.'

'Shouldn't have to lecture you about rationing your food, after all you're not a baby.'

Krokr Longtoe winged low across the field and pitched up into a tall ash as Sabrax and Dorcan got up from their meal. He shook his tail and bobbed his head as he watched the two Clykes gather up their things. The brothers looked around warily, scanned the treetops and, seeing nothing untoward, set off again. Krokr waited until they were out of sight before he slipped from the tree and flew after them.

Dorcan whistled as he walked along in the warm sunshine. He was elated now that he and his brother were well on the way home. He thought about the welcome they'd get. A great fuss would be made of them. Heroes, that's what they'd be. Everyone would be there to shout their names and cheer them. A big spread of food and gallons of nettle beer would be laid on - his stomach rumbled.

'Hang on.' Sabrax lowered his bag and line to the ground.

'What's up?'

'Up? Nothing's up. Just want to have a quick look round.'

Dorcan sat down on a nearby stone, idly twirling a dock

leaf between his finger and thumb as Sabrax scaled the wall.

'Well?' said Dorcan, gazing up to where his brother stood on the camstones.

'I can see the stone circle.'

'Great. How far away is it?'

Dorcan got up and stood on the stone.

'We should reach it midday tomorrow at the latest and then it's all downhill to our walls.'

A dark shadow passed over Sabrax. Shielding his eyes with his hand, he glanced up at the sun. He dropped his hand and looked to the ground below. His brother had gone.

'Dorcs? Dorcan?' shouted Sabrax, a note of anxiety in his voice. He scrambled down from the wall. 'Where are you?' he bellowed. 'Stop messing about. It's not funny. If you're hiding . . . '

Sabrax stood and listened for a moment.

'Dor-can? Where are you?'

Sabrax's mouth was dry. He began to search among the grasses and look under bushes, but there was no sign of his brother.

'Dor-can,' he shouted again.

Then Sabrax saw it, a single, brown and white mottled flight feather lying beside the track. He picked it up.

'No. Not that. No, please no. He doesn't deserve that. Such a good little Clyke.'

Sabrax hurled the feather away.

*

118

Chapter Twelve

Longalio was alone in Long Hall. He stood at the table, studying the large piece of potato bag paper spread in front of him, on which he'd drawn his layout for the Clykes' display at the Craft Show. Every year since anyone can remember, at midnight, under the first full moon after the harvest, Clykes and the other wall-dwellers from the surrounding area met in an old ruined tower sited on a hillside near the old mill. Here they would enter their work for the many different competitions, everything from best beeswax to most useful item made from a reused tin. It was a chance to demonstrate their craft skills to others. The Clykes had always been successful at the show in the past and their awards, gold oak sprays and silver laurel leaf crests, hung on the walls in Long Hall. Longalio had been looking forward to the show this year, certain that Calamorica's family could do well with several of their exhibits. Calamorica, however, hadn't expressed any enthusiasm for anything, including the show, since the disastrous encounter with the hawk and the loss of the talisman. The door to Long Hall opened. Longalio glanced across. It was Durabito who came in.

'Any news of Sabrax and Dorcan?'

'The swallows can't find them,' said Durabito, 'vanished into thin air. They're still searching.'

'And Calamorica?'

'Looks as though she's given up.'

'Oh my goodness, no.'

'The others have noticed it too. Not something you can conceal, is it? She's muttering in her sleep now - asking to see Cantardio.'

'It's all quite frightening,' croaked Longalio, lowering himself into his chair, 'like a slowly developing illness. It'll finish us all off.'

Durabito studied the sheet of paper on the table.

'Entries? For this year's show? Do you think we should go? You know, with our problem and all?'

'If we don't, it's going to look odd. Provoke a few questions, get malicious tongues wagging.'

'But how do we account for those among us who are missing?'

*

Grief had taken Sabrax. He'd sat and wept for Dorcan and now he'd run out of tears. He struggled to his feet. He hid Dorcan's bag and line in a gap in the wall and clapped the dust from his hands. He marked the place with a sprig of yellow gorse

'Must get on,' he muttered, 'got to get home.'

He slid his bag and line over his shoulder and, head

down, set off along the track again. He did not hear the insects flying or the bees about their work or the sheep baa-ing on the fell. He did not see the bright sun, or the white clouds as they bubbled up in a clear blue sky, or the flowers and grasses in the fields. Nor was he aware of the great black bird that had flown towards him and settled on the wall.

'What's the matter?'

Sabrax looked up. A glossy raven gazed down at him from the wall top.

'Nothing.'

'Look at you - walking along in a daze. What has happened that makes you appear so forlorn?'

'My brother, my brother's missing.'

'I see.'

'Taken by a hawk.'

'Are you sure?'

'I found a hawk's flight feather. He was there one minute and gone the next. Just like that.' Sabrax clicked his fingers.

'Where were you going?'

'We were on our way home.'

'Where had you been?'

'To Mailcann Forest.'

'What for?'

'To find something and recover it.'

'What?'

'Our brooch.'

Sabrax closed his eyes and his chin sank to his chest when he realised what he had said.

'There. Now all the other tribes will know of our carelessness.'

'I won't tell anyone. Your secret is safe with me. But how can I help you, that's the thing?'

'I don't think you can help. Everything was going so well. Our journey was almost over. And now . . . '

'Yes?'

'I'll have to go. I must keep going.'

Sabrax started walking again.

'What prevents you from staying and searching for your brother?' the raven called after him. 'This brooch you talked about, is that it?'

'Yes.'

The raven launched itself from the wall, flew along to where Sabrax stood and landed again.

'So. You want to stay, but you need to go. I can help you.'

'How?'

'If I asked you to believe in what I can do, would you believe and let me help?'

'Helped by a raven?'

'I'm no ordinary bird; I can assure you of that. I know many things. Now, let me see the brooch.'

Sabrax took his handkerchief from his pocket. He unfolded it carefully and showed the sparkling talisman to the raven.

'It's been in our family for generations and always kept us safe from harm. Cataporinganio said . . . '

'Cataporinganio?'

'He's a wizard.'

'What's he like?'

'Strong, wise, clever - the cleverest in all the world, I believe.'

'Really?' said the raven.

'The brooch, it's our tribe's talisman. If we were to lose it and not recover it, disaster would strike. We might all die. I don't understand how it works, but we know it does.'

'I see. Now will you do something for me? Extend your arm and show the brooch in the palm of your open hand.'

'What for?'

'Just do it, Sabrax, that's all I ask.'

Sabrax did as he was bid. He held out his arm and opened his hand.

'How do you know my name?'

*

Calamorica sat in silence at the table. Several Clykes were with her, to keep her company.

'Try and eat something,' said Durahito.

'Not really hungry,' said Calamorica, laying down her spoon and pushing the bowl of soup away.

She took her napkin from around her neck, folded it loosely and dropped it on the table. Calamorica got up as though to walk away, then sat down again and stared straight ahead. The Clykes looked at each other and then back towards Calamorica.

'Look, look there,' cried Longalio in horror.

A sparkling red jewel had begun to appear out of thin air in the middle of the table. Clykes scattered in terror and ran to the four corners of the room. Calamorica remained seated, watching in silence as a gold setting slowly surrounded the stone.

'The brooch,' she whispered, 'but how?'

Durabito walked over and stood behind Calamorica's chair.

'Is it possible, sister?'

Calamorica leaned forward, picked up the precious brooch and clasped it to her chest.

'It's back. It's real. It's come home. Our talisman has come home to us. But where are Sabrax and Dorcan?'

*

'Vanished,' bellowed Sabrax, 'what have you done with it?'

'The brooch is safely home, back with your family.'

'How do I know that?' He drew his knife. 'If you have tricked me.'

'There's no trick. In time you'll see.'

'It can't simply disappear.'

'No, indeed. You've things to do, Sabrax. Put your knife away. And if you want to see your brother again, you must obey my instructions.'

'If Dorcan alive is the prize, I will.'

*

'Help me,' shouted Durabito, 'here, quick, help me, Calamorica's ill.'

Clykes ran into Long Hall from all directions and gathered round. She lay face down on the table, the brooch still in her hand. The Clykes raised her up, taking great care as they lifted her from her chair and carried her out through Long Hall and into her bedroom. Longalio ran to the potions cupboard. He got out a small bottle and dashed to the kitchen. There he mixed three drops into a small cup of water and took the draught into Calamorica's bedroom.

'Longalio? What happened?' whispered Calamorica.

'You fainted. Now here, drink this.' He held the cup to Calamorica's lips. 'It'll make you sleep. You've been worrying far too much.'

Calamorica swallowed the draught and lay back again. Durabito straightened her pillows.

'Sabrax, Dor… can,' Calamorica's lids grew heavy as the potion began to work, 'we must find them, we must . . .'

'Rest and sleep, sister' said Durabito, 'we'll work something out, never fear.'

*

'What now, Raven?' asked Sabrax, picking up his bag and line and swinging them over his shoulder.

'I want you to follow me. Follow until I tell you otherwise.'

'Lead on.'

Spreading its wings, the raven flew from the wall top. Sabrax strode off after it. He ran among the grasses through the middle of a haymeadow, glancing up at the raven whenever it drifted into view, its glossy feathers lit by the sun. The bird would circle high over his head, fly on then return to hover over him again. The raven maintained this pattern of flight all the while, leading Sabrax on through haymeadows and fields of barley. It was late afternoon when the raven called to him.

'Sabrax. Here. This is the way.'

Sabrax travelled through a tunnel of thick brambles,

emerging by a gated wall that enclosed another haymeadow. A corncrake's *crek*, *crek*, *crek* call rose up. Sabrax smiled on hearing the familiar cry, for he remembered this strange bird of his childhood as it crept among the flowers and grasses, seeking a mate. He stooped under the bottom bar of the gate and walked arrow-straight across the meadow to another gate on the far side that stood open onto a stonefield.

'Not far now,' encouraged the raven, 'make your way across this last tract.'

Sabrax followed a faint way among the stones that led him on over the edge of a great limestone scar and zigzagged down a steep slope. As he slithered and slid over the loose scree, Sabrax gazed up at the scar face. Stunted whitebeams and junipers grew in fantastic shapes, their roots anchored deep in rock fissures. Some of the juniper bushes were tall and pointed, others spread out in long green fingers. Great clumps of yellow rockroses and purple cranesbills hung in drifts from the narrow ledges. All the time, as Sabrax negotiated the difficult descent, the raven drifted overhead, watching anxiously. Grazed and bruised, Sabrax reached the bottom of the cliffs.

'Go left,' called the circling raven.

Sabrax continued along the foot of the scar until he reached the edge of a wood of ash, hazel and holly.

'Is this the place, Raven?' he shouted.

The bird began to lose height.

'Nearly there.'

Sabrax entered the wood, the raven now flying only a few feet above him. He arrived at a small clearing where two roe deer grazed with their fawns. The animals

126

looked up from feeding to watch this little creature and a huge black bird pass by.

'We have arrived at our destination,' said the raven, landing on a rock outcrop. The bird pointed with a wing tip to a great cleft in the rock wall. 'You must pass through there. Don't be afraid. I'll follow you.'

Going across to the narrow opening in the limestone, Sabrax went in. He emerged in a hidden gorge surrounded by high walls of solid rock. A great stream of water poured out of a fissure in the limestone and fell into a deep, clear pool. He could see small pieces of broken crockery and the many coins that lay on the bottom. Short strips of cloth and linen hung from the branches of the hazel trees that grew there. The outlet stream from the pool ran in a deep channel in the rock and disappeared underground beneath a large flat stone. Sabrax studied the strange designs and devices, hollows, whorls and rings that were carved on the stone's surface.

'Raven? Is this the work of Talluns?'

'It is.'

'What does it all mean?'

'They are star maps.'

Sabrax ran his finger around the grooved outline of a whorl cut in the stone. The stone began to glow with a mysterious radiance. He pulled his finger away and it faded.

He glanced up at the raven; it looked surprised.

'Do stones do that usually?'

'Not usually, they don't, no. No. No, they don't,' the raven mused, 'only when they are touched by a . . . a certain individual. Even I didn't expect that to happen. Still, we must get on. Now, under the stone,' he pointed to it with the tip of his wing, 'there is a well. You must immerse yourself in its water.'

'Why?'

'It will enable you to withstand great pain.'

'There's to be more suffering?'

'It's the way, I'm afraid. It's always been like this.'

'How do I get into the well?' asked Sabrax, 'I can't move that stone by myself.'

'You won't have to. Stand clear.'

Sabrax did as the raven bade and moved out of the way. The bird lowered its head and stared at the carved stone. Sabrax watched wide-eyed. The great stone remained immobile for a few seconds then it budged a little before sliding and moving away with a great echoing rumble. Sabrax walked to the edge of the well head and stared into its depths. He picked up a pebble and tossed it down. After several moments, he heard a distinct plop from far below.

'I'm to go down there?'

'Yes.'

Sabrax tied his line to the trunk of a hazel growing by the spring. He pulled hard on the line to test the knot and cast the rest of the coil down into the well. Standing at the well head, he gripped the line, gave it a final tug and, satisfied that it was secure, stepped over the edge.

*

Chapter Thirteen

Longalio carried a basket filled with logs. He pushed open the door to Long Hall with his foot, went in and set the basket down by the hearth. Glancing sideways, he noticed a folded sheet of flour bag paper on the table. Curious, he went across and picked it up. Durabito shuffled into Long Hall.

'Looks like a message. Someone's left a message.'

'Who's it for?' asked Durabito.

'Don't know. No name on it.'

Longalio unfolded the paper and glanced at the message written in the neat strokes, dots, squiggles and whorls of Clyke script.

'Oh my goodness, it's for us.'

'Read it out.'

'What?'

'Read the message out,' said Durabito.

'Of course - read it out.'

Longalio cleared his throat.

Uncle Longalio and Durabito
We have decided to go and look for Sabrax and Dorcan.
Don't be concerned. The swallows will take care of us and help us find our brothers.
Love
Rosmanda and Woadica

'Gone.' Longalio laid the paper down on the table.
'That's what it says.'
'Do you think it's wise, their going like that?'
'You know what they're like - once they get an idea into their heads.'
'Headstrong those two.'
'Very,' said Durabito.
'We'd never catch up with them.'
'No. Besides it would leave no one in charge.'
'Yes, that's it,' said Longalio, nodding, 'we're needed here, to keep an eye on things.'

*

Rosmanda and Woadica moved swiftly through the grasses at the edge of a wood. Rosmanda had a crossbow slung across her back. Hung on metal loops on her wide leather belt were a long knife in a sheath, a quiver of crossbow bolts and her mustard pouch. Her hair was gathered in a knot on her neck. The two sisters both wore long brown boots and shirts and trousers of green and brown. A sheath knife and a mustard pouch hung from Woadica's belt and over her shoulder she carried a canvas bag. Rosmanda stopped suddenly and knelt down.

'Look here,' she said, gesturing at the print of a boot in the soft earth.

Woadica knelt down beside her. She looked closely at the print. 'Sabrax, definitely. I'd recognise those sole marks anywhere.'

The sisters stood up. They searched around and soon found other small signs - a broken twig, a bent blade of grass and a crab apple core, thrown away, no doubt, by Dorcan.

'Thanks for the signs,' said Rosmanda, 'don't worry boys, we'll find you.'

*

Sabrax was halfway down the well by the time he paused for a moment to rest. He glanced up to the opening far above and even though it was still early afternoon, he saw that the sky beyond the well head had grown dark. He wriggled on the rope and eased himself into a more comfortable position to continue his descent. He made to set off again, but on his very first step down, his foot slipped on a patch of slime. His knees slammed into the sharp stones jutting from the well side, the violent jolt knocking the climbing line from his grip. He seized the line again, but it ripped through his hands and burned the skin off his palms and fingers as he struggled to arrest his fall. Unable to stand the excruciating pain, he let go. He dropped down and down and down into the darkness.

'No-ooooooooooooo.'

At the bottom of the well, Sabrax hit the ice-cold water and went deep under, the water glooping and fizzing around him. He kicked frantically with his feet and flailed his arms, his lungs feeling as though they were about to burst. He broke through the surface and gulped in air. Coughing and spluttering, he swam to the side of the well where he found a crack in the rock and clung to it. The water chilled him to the bone. Sabrax looked back up. A long way above him, beyond the 'O' of the well head, the sky was black and studded with stars. He knew that it was daylight outside and yet from here, in the depths of this well, he was able to see a night sky. He swam around the well sides seeking his line and, to his great joy, found it straight away. He pulled himself clear of the surface and hung on the line for a moment, waiting for the freezing water to drain from him.

'Now then,' he muttered, 'get out, come on, you can do it.'

He took a firm hold on the line and began the long haul up and out of the well.

*

The curtains in Calamorica's bedroom were drawn. Durabito and Longalio sat quietly on either side of their sister's bed. Durabito pressed a wet cloth to Calamorica's forehead as the old Clyke mumbled in her sleep.

'Is it a fever?' asked Longalio.

Durabito pulled the cloth away and dipped it again in a bucket of cold spring water.

'No, it's not a fever,' he said, sitting back in his chair, 'far worse than that I'm afraid.'

'Oh?'

'I've seen this before, many years ago.'

'What is it?'

'I'm afraid Calamorica's given up the will to live.'

'What?'

'She's decided to turn her head to the wall and pass over.'

'Oh my goodness,' said Longalio, 'why?'

'The worry provoked by the loss of the talisman, coupled with Sabrax and Dorcan going missing, has taken its toll. She's tired. She's had enough.'

*

Sabrax rested for a moment on a step in the well side to get his breath back. The stars beyond the well head had long since vanished into the glare of the day and now a shaft of strong sunlight shone down. Sabrax stared at his hands and saw that they were burned and blistered, but did not hurt. It was then that he remembered the reason for him being here in the well. Hadn't the raven said that once he had been immersed in the water he wouldn't feel pain?

'Are you all right?'

Sabrax looked up. He saw the raven staring down at him.

'Yes, fine.'

'You were immersed in the water?'

'Yes.'

'Good, that's very good. Climb on.'

Sabrax began to climb again and soon reached the top. He pulled himself up and out of the well. He rolled over on the ground and lay still. The raven saw Sabrax staring at his calloused and blistered hands.

'Raven?'

'Yes.'

'Why did I have to go to the water at the bottom of the well? Wouldn't it have been easier for me to bathe in the spring up here?'

'At the bottom of the well, did you notice anything - unusual?'

'The water was icy cold.'

'Apart from that.'

'I could see the stars in a black sky.'

'Exactly. Starlight and spring water. It's a powerful combination. The strength of starlight diminishes at night, but it doubles in the daytime. You have bathed in the water and starlight, it should ensure you survive in extreme situations.'

'How long will my hands be free of pain?' Sabrax held them up for the raven to see.

'Until the next full moon. Your hands will be healed by then.'

Sabrax pulled his line up out of the depths of the well, wound it into a coil and stood back from the edge. The raven stared again at the great flat stone. He locked it in his gaze. With a mighty rumble, the stone began to slide and covered the well once more.

'What now, Raven?'

'The difficult bit, I'm afraid. You will have to let this hawk catch you. Then you must kill it.'

'Caught by the hawk and then kill it?'

The raven roused its feathers then spoke in a measured tone.

'You have shown your bravery in the past, Sabrax. Will

you do this?'

'It will bring Dorcan back?'

'It will.'

'And if I fail?'

'You'll not fail.'

Sabrax stared at the ground and thought what it must be like to be seized by a hawk.

'I'll do it.'

'Good. A true Clyke.' The raven roused its feathers again. 'Now, come along with me. What you need is the weapon for the deed. I know a place not far from here where you will find it.'

Closely watched by the raven, Sabrax clambered over the rubbish tip at the back of a nearby farm. It was early evening now and he had been at this task for several hours.

'Like looking for a grain of sand in a leaf pile, only smellier.'

'Keep at it, Sabrax, you'll find it soon enough.'

Sabrax dragged rotten wooden boards, broken boxes and large empty tins out of his way. He moved with great care among discarded metal and plastic containers from which tiny iridescent chemical rivers oozed to merge with the black liquor from old silage bags. It was then he spotted that which he sought, a syringe for injecting cattle. The plastic body had a plunger at one end and a sharp needle at the other. Sabrax picked it up. He pulled the shiny needle from the tube and held it aloft for the raven to see.

'Is this it?'

'Well done. Now you have your weapon.'

'Why this and not my axe?'

'Feel the weight of it. Go on.'

Sabrax wafted the needle about in his hand and held it at arm's length, then lunged forward, jabbing the air.

'Well?'

'Light as a feather,' said Sabrax.

'Hollow, but twice as strong as a flat blade.'

Birds were going to their roosts and the first stars had emerged in the darkening sky. Sabrax sat under a rowan tree at the pool by the well. With his knife he'd carved a handle from a piece of ash. Now he was fixing it to the hollow needle. He eased the handle onto the needle and beat it on a stone several times. It was a tight fit. He grasped the handle. Now he had the sword for the task.

'Well done,' said the raven, 'now, take your sword to the edge of the pool and cast it in.'

Doing as the raven asked, he walked to the edge of the pool and threw in his sword. It sank beneath the surface in a swirl of bubbles.

'Now you must walk round the pool three times in the direction of the sun.'

Under the raven's watchful gaze, Sabrax walked three times around the pool.

'You can get your sword now.'

Sabrax plunged his arm into the water and retrieved his sword. He dried it with his shirtsleeve and leaned the sword against a large limestone boulder. He looked to the place where the raven sat, but the dark bird had slipped away.

Sabrax found safe shelter for the night high up in a cleft

in a limestone outcrop. He was weary now and ready for sleep. Deep inside, he felt a state of calm he had never known before, his mind flooded with soothing voices. He climbed into his sleeping sack and lay back on his pillow of boots and line. He stared for a while at the moonlit surfaces and dark shadows in the landscape. His thoughts drifted to his family at home.

'May it all go well tomorrow. I love you, all.'

Sabrax's eyes grew heavy. He turned over in his sack. In no time at all, sleep took him.

*

'They'll all be in their beds by now at home, enjoying peaceful sleep after a busy day,' said Woadica, turning over and trying another position in which to sleep.

'Have you been thinking about Sabrax and Dorcan a lot today? I know I have.'

'Yes, I have. Much more than I'd normally do. At home you take them for granted, don't you?'

'Mmmm.'

'Part of us, flesh and blood.'

Rosmanda moved restlessly.

'Wish I could find a piece of ground as soft as my mattress at home.'

'Know what you mean, my back's killing me,' said Woadica.

A tawny owl hooted from its perch high up in an ash.

'Listen to it. I'm glad we're in here. I wouldn't feel safe out there with such a big killer on the loose, those cruel talons closing on you.'

'Don't,' said Woadica, 'I'm frightened enough as it is.'

The owl hooted again.

'Coming closer - and it's going to eat you.'

Rosmanda placed her curled fingers on Woadica's head and shrieked out loud.

'Eeeeeeeekkkkk.'

At the top of the tree, the owl swung its head round and its sharp eyes scanned the wall below.

*

Chapter Fourteen

Sabrax opened his eyes. It was already dawn. Birds were singing to welcome in the day. He wriggled out of his sleeping sack and got up. He began to pack his belongings. He was tired of sleeping rough and longed for a good hot bath and some clean clothes. Picking up his tree axe, he slid off its canvas cover. He looked at his distorted reflection in the shining blade. The axe had served him well, he mused, as indeed it had served other Clykes, since being forged by an elf smith many years ago.

'Not today, old friend, sleep for you.'

Sabrax slid the cover back over the axe head. He wrapped the axe up in a piece of cloth and stowed it in his bag. After he'd pulled on his boots, he packed his climbing gear and reached for his new sword. He swung it above his head and leapt forward, cutting and thrusting the empty air.

'Well, my new companion, today we will see if you are as lethal as old friend axe.'

He went from his shelter in the limestone out into the bright morning. The raven was there and gazed down at him from its perch on the rock.

'A fine day, for righting a great wrong.'

'That's why I'm here,' replied Sabrax, 'to carry the day.'

He held his new sword aloft before running forward and practising two handed fighting. He leapt over and away from imaginary blades.

'A hawk, remember, not an enemy wielding a sword.'

Sabrax dropped the sword to his side.

'You will get just one chance to kill it, and you must do it in one thrust.'

*

From his perch high up in an ash tree, Krokr Longtoe watched Rosmanda and Woadica as they walked on the track below. When the sisters were directly underneath the tree, Krokr leapt off the branch through the curtain of leaves, folded his wings and streaked towards them. Rosmanda heard the wind noise from Krokr's vibrating feathers. She glanced up in time to see the hawk as it stooped down at her.

'Hawk! Hawk! Watch out!'

Woadica threw herself to the ground. In an instant, Rosmanda had reached into her mustard pouch, drawn out a handful of powder and hurled it at Krokr. He was enveloped in a billowing yellow cloud. Rosmanda screamed loudly and clapped her hands. This was enough to unnerve Krokr, for he pulled out of his stoop, flew up sharply and winged away.

'Ros?'

'I'm all right.'

Woadica got to her feet. She beat the dust from her clothes. Rosmanda pulled her crossbow strap over her head, put her foot in the bow's metal stirrup, drew back the string and clicked on the trigger. From her quiver she got a bolt and set the knock on the string. She held the crossbow level with both hands at waist height.

'We've got to be more alert, Woad, otherwise we're hawk food.'

'Do you think that's what's happened to . . . ?'

Woadica realised what she was saying. She looked at her sister.

*

It was quiet in the darkened bedroom. Longalio and Durabito stood either side of Calamorica's bed. Bunches of flowers in all manner of containers filled every available surface and the air was heavy with their perfume. The brothers had watched a candle set in a holder on Calamorica's bedside table suddenly gutter and go out. Durabito pulled Calamorica's hand out from under the bed covers and held his own hand on Calamorica's wrist.

'Well?' said Longalio.

'She's gone, there's no pulse.'

*

'No. No!'

'What is it?' asked the raven. 'What's the matter?'

Sabrax stood up. He was wide eyed and agitated. He

walked to the edge of the pool.

'Something's happened.' Sabrax glanced about in his alarm. 'See. There. By the hazels, look.' He pointed to the trees at the pool. 'See. It's my mother. Mother, it's me, Sabrax.'

'There's no one there,' said the raven.

Sabrax stared fixedly at the hazels for some minutes. Finally he shook his head.

'You're overwrought.'

'Yes. You are right, Raven. It is nothing. There is no one there. I'm imagining things. A trick of the light. It is nothing.'

*

The official bearers among the Clykes had carried Calamorica's body to the middle of a field and laid it out on the ground in accordance with their custom, to await burial by the sexton beetles. Now they were strewing fresh flowers around her.

'Come on, everyone,' said Longalio, 'it's time for us to go.'

Several Clykes still came forward to whisper their sad farewells to Calamorica and leave their own small bunches of flowers. Some of the Clykes stood about in the grass, looking forlorn. With heads bowed, the main group walked back across the field towards their wall. Longalio and Durabito brushed tears from their eyes as they waited behind for one last look at their sister.

'What a disaster,' whispered Longalio, 'she's gone, and all her children missing. They know nothing of this. Calamorica, I loved you,' he leaned over and stroked her hair, 'you were the best sister anyone could have wished for.' He dabbed his eyes with a handkerchief and moved away.

'Goodbye, Calamorica,' said Durabito, 'sleep well, sister.' Durabito wiped his eyes with the back of his hand and began his slow walk to where his brother stood.

'Saddest day of my life,' said Durabito sniffing.

'Mine too,' said Longalio.

*

'Look. Here, and there,' cried Woadica, pointing to several boot prints impressed in the soft earth.

'There are more over here, Woad. And these scrapes on the ground, they've been made by boots, too. Look.'

Rosmanda pointed to a single flight feather caught up in a patch of gorse. Woadica pulled the feather out from the spiny plant. She laid it flat on the ground and studied the feather's markings.

'I get a cold sensation from it, something awful has happened here.'

Woadica stood up and with her arms outstretched, closed her eyes and began a high-pitched chant. Rosmanda searched among the grasses and bushes in a wide arc around the wall. She stopped suddenly. Woadica halted in mid-chant and opened her eyes. Rosmanda leaned forward and got something from the grasses. She turned to her sister and held up a boot.

'Dorcan's,' said Woadica.

*

'Remember, you will feel the great blow from the hawk's feet and you will be in shock after it takes you.'

Sabrax nodded slowly, listening carefully to what the raven was saying.

'You'll be winded and the talons will stab, but you will feel no pain.'

'When should I kill the hawk?'

'The hawk will carry you straight to its plucking post to kill and eat you. So as soon as it lands, you'll have one clear chance and no more. Do you understand?'

'Yes. I'll do it, never fear.'

'I have complete faith in you. Now, it's time. Get yourself ready, become honed to your task.'

'Clykes away,' roared Sabrax.

He raised his new sword above his head, sunlight glinting on the hollow blade.

'Clykes away,' said the raven.

Sabrax pushed the sword inside his belt and climbed up to the top of the wall. He got to his feet among the camstones and stood for a moment looking out over the haymeadows. They were the best he'd seen in a long time. Tall grasses waved to and fro in the breeze, while flowers showed their heads among the stalks. He gazed up, his eyes resting on the deep blue sky streaked by long fingers of white cloud.

'So beautiful,' he whispered, 'all of it. So beautiful.'

He fastened his shirt buttons, pulled his belt in a notch and practised drawing his sword with his right hand. The raven flew across. It joined him on the wall top.

'I can't give you any more help, at least not until the hawk is dead.'

'I won't let anyone down.'

'I know,' said the raven, nodding, 'good luck.'

The raven leapt from the wall. It circled about in the air, flew off towards a tall ash and landed on the topmost branch.

Sabrax cut a solitary figure atop the wall. He hummed snatches of an old Clyke tune to keep his spirits up and thought it was such a fine day to be taken by a hawk.

'Look at me, Hawk, wherever you are. Sabrax Clyke, hawk-bait,' he shouted, 'Sabrax Clyke, hawk-lure.'

Then he heard the familiar cries of the swallows. He saw the birds flashing and darting over the walls as they sped towards him. The birds reached Sabrax and gathered in the air above his head as they twittered excitedly, 'Sabrax, Sabrax'.

'Out of here, get out of here, if you know what's good for you,' Sabrax yelled.

He waved his arms and watched the small flock of swallows as they sped away.

Drawn by the small birds' cries, Krokr Longtoe was already powering his way over the haymeadows.

*

'Look, look,' shouted Rosmanda. 'Swallows. They've found us.'

The small flock of swallows flew nearer and nearer and within seconds hovered over the sisters' heads, twittering excitedly.

'Where are Sabrax and Dorcan? Where?' begged Woadica.

'Sabrax's here, Sabrax's here,' cried the swallows.

The birds flew back the way they had come.

'Follow them. Look, they want us to follow them,' yelled Rosmanda.

She ran after the birds.

'Ros, wait. Wait for me.'

*

Sabrax felt the sharp talons close around him. He was winded, for the hawk's strike was as violent as the raven had predicted. Now Krokr was carrying him along at a great rate through the air, Sabrax struggling to regain his senses as the wind roared over him and the ground flashed by below, his arms pinned tightly to his side by the locked talons. He tried to wrest a hand free and seize the sword handle, but could only touch it with the tip of a finger. Krokr felt the movement and gripped Sabrax harder. He made no attempt to land or to eat his prey as he rose up in the sky.

'No,' croaked the raven, staring at Krokr wheeling up towards the clouds, 'this is all wrong. What on earth is it doing?'

Sabrax felt dizzy and closed his eyes, as the ground below rotated under him.

'Not how it should be,' he muttered, 'not like this at all.'

He was beyond help now, and he knew it. He could feel Krokr's straining chest muscles hard against him as they drove the wings up and down. Krokr climbed higher in the sky and panted with the effort. For a brief moment he spread his wings and soared on the thermals rising from the hot fields below. Krokr opened his beak wide. He gulped in mouthfuls of air. Sabrax felt faint.

He couldn't move his fingers and his hands were beginning to grow cold.

The raven followed the hawk's flight from its vantage point at the top of the ash. He, too, knew that Sabrax was beyond help; the brave Clyke was doomed. The raven sighed and lowered its head. Then something - even the raven did not know what - caused it to glance up at the hawk again. As he stared at the bird of prey high overhead, the raven's eyes widened, for the hawk appeared to falter in flight.

Krokr Longtoe had heard the hiss and felt the impact. Now something was lodged deep within his body. He was trapped in his nightmare. A great pain seared his chest. Blood seeped from the corner of his beak. Suddenly a great weariness washed over him. His muscles failed; his wings faltered on the down stroke and would not rise for the upstroke. His breathing was shallow. He tried to gulp in air. Krokr struggled to stay aloft. He opened his talons.

'You've hit it. Ros, you've hit it.'

Rosmanda lowered her crossbow and saw the hawk stall in the air. The sisters had arrived in time to see their brother snatched from the wall. Rosmanda had trained her crossbow on the bird, waited until she'd a clear view and fired the bolt. Now the stricken killer was on its way down, streaking to earth in a pluming stream of small body feathers.

'Any sign of Sabrax?'

'I can't see him. Come on, let's be there when the hawk comes down.'

Sabrax felt Krokr's grip on him lessen, watching the sharp talons unfold and the hawk slip away.

'Heeeeeeelllllllllllllppppppppppp,' Sabrax shrieked, as he dropped through the air.

He began to roll over and over. He could not see, his eyes streamed as the wind raced and roared around him. He extended his hands, his arms and then his legs into a star shape in an attempt to slow his fall. Though he no longer tumbled over and over in this position, it did nothing to lessen the speed at which he plunged to earth. As the ground rushed up to meet him he shut his eyes tight and shouted.

'I did my best. Aaaaaaaaaaaaaaaaaaaaaaaaaaaaa.'

The raven fixed Sabrax in its gaze.

Sabrax noticed straight away that the wind noise had gone. He opened his eyes and saw that the fields no longer rushed up towards him. He was suddenly filled with hope, realising that he was *floating* through the air, floating, not hurtling. He began to whistle loudly but stopped mid-tune to watch Krokr hit the ground far below and tumble over and over in a cloud of feathers and dust.

Woadica and Rosmanda reached the spot where the hawk had crash-landed. The bird lay on its back in a ragged heap, wings smashed and feathers broken. Both of the bird's feet were open. Of Sabrax there was no sign.

'Where is he?'

'He must be here,' said Rosmanda, 'he must.'

'Sabrax, Sabrax,' shouted Woadica.

The sisters ran about in a frantic search for him, ranging over a wide area around the place where the hawk lay.

'Sabrax, Sabrax,' Woadica shouted again, 'where are

you?'

Only silence greeted the two Clykes.

'Oh Sabrax, I'm sorry,' yelled Rosmanda, 'I shouldn't have fired the bolt. You're dead. You're dead. I know it.'

She leaned against a tree root, buried her head in her hands and started sobbing. Woadica came over and put an arm around her sister and stroked her hair.

'You had no choice. I'd have done the same. The hawk was taking him to his death - no doubt about it. He must be here somewhere.'

Rosmanda struggled to compose herself and stood wiping away her tears with the back of her hand, sniffing all the while.

'Sab-rax,' she bellowed, at the top of her voice, her throat and lungs straining with the effort.

'Heeeelllloooooo.'

'Woad?'

Woadica raised her eyes skywards.

'You just have to see this.'

Rosmanda looked up. Sabrax was drifting like a feather in the air.

'Rosmanda, Woadica, look at me. Wheeeeeee.'

Sabrax spiralled down and down and down. He saw his sisters' faces, eyes wide and mouths open. He landed on his feet near to where they stood.

'You were flying,' yelled Woadica, as she and Rosmanda ran to him and threw their arms around him.

'Flying,' said Rosmanda, 'like a bird. But how?'

Sabrax gazed up at the ash tree. The topmost branch was empty. He drew his sword and tossed it away.

'Complete waste of time that. I was supposed to kill

the hawk with it.'

'Ros killed it, with a crossbow bolt,' said Woadica.

'My clever sisters,' exclaimed Sabrax, hugging them. 'I hope you'll forgive me, Ros, for brushing you off when you wanted to come with me and help retrieve the brooch. What brilliant Clykes you are.'

Sabrax hugged them again. Then the three were wrapped in a long silent embrace.

'Where's Dorcan?' asked Rosmanda suddenly.

Sabrax sighed.

'Where is he?' said Rosmanda again.

Sabrax stared at the ground.

'The hawk got him.'

Woadica and Rosmanda groaned out an agonised, 'Nooo.' Tears filled their eyes and they began to sob. Soon Sabrax was weeping too.

'I don't believe it,' cried Woadica, 'our little Dorcan.'

'It's true,' said Sabrax, 'I let him down. I promised him he'd be safe.'

A dishevelled figure appeared out of the bushes behind the three Clykes. It staggered for a moment, straightened up and walked towards them.

'Yawwwnnnn. Ahhhhmmm.'

'Dorcan?' said Sabrax, turning round.

The three Clykes rushed to Dorcan and seized and hugged him.

'My baby brother, you've come back,' moaned Woadica.

'Living and breathing,' marvelled Rosmanda.

'You're alive,' said Sabrax in disbelief.

'Course I am. What time of day is it?'

'Never mind that.'

'What are Rosmanda and Woadica doing here? I've lost

a boot. Anyone seen my boot?'
  'Where have you come from?' asked Sabrax.
  'I've come from where you've come from - the forest.'
  'No, I mean now, where have you come from now?'
  'I've been sleeping. Haven't you?'

*

It was lunchtime and the mood around the table in Long
Hall was sombre. Longalio had been busy in the kitchen
all morning. He'd got out the old recipe book and had
cooked the Clykes' favourite food. He'd made corn
pancakes, pignut broth, fennel and fern casserole, deep-
fried nettle leaves, crab apple fritters, potato and cheese
wedges, beech mast shapes, honey and blackcurrant tart
and oatmeal toasties. It was a great display of Longalio's
skills and applauded by the other Clykes. But even this
grand selection of their favourite things could not raise
their spirits. Clykes sat glumly at the table and picked at
the food with their forks. Nobody felt like eating.
  Later in the afternoon, most of the Clykes were still in
Long Hall. Some were sitting in silence reading books,
or looking out of the windows, while others sat in chairs
staring vacantly into space. Durabito came into the
room.
  'I know you're not going to believe this, but look who
I've found out in the field.'
  Nobody looked up or turned around at first. Longalio
broke off from reading his book. He glanced up.
  'Calamorica.'
  Longalio turned to his book again. After a moment a
look of surprise and terror crossed his face.

'Calamorica - aaaaggghhhh. A spirit. A spirit. Look, look!'

Clykes leapt to their feet and soon the room was in uproar.

'Silly beggars,' said Calamorica.

She ambled across to the table and helped herself to a deep-fried nettle leaf.

'I'm starving, feel as though I haven't eaten for a week.'

'You're alive,' said Longalio.

'Of course I am.'

'We laid you out.'

'What on earth for?'

'You'd died.'

'Are you feeling all right?'

'I don't know any more,' said Longalio, 'I'm confused.'

'You're confused? What about me? Suddenly to wake up in the middle of a field, bedecked in flowers and wearing my best dress.'

*

Chapter Fifteen

Within Long Hall, Clykes had filled every available chair and were packed tight around the supper table, like slow-worms in a wall in spring. Sabrax, Rosmanda, Woadica and Calamorica sat together.

'A bird?' said Calamorica, 'you say you were helped by a bird?'

'Yes,' said Sabrax, 'it was a very wise old bird. It could talk Clyke. It caused our talisman to disappear, and reappear here. It had strange powers, knew everything, and even knew my name. The bird could move things just by looking at them. The stone over the secret well, for example.'

'A secret well?' whispered Calamorica, staring at Sabrax.

'Yes, it showed me a secret . . . '

There was a loud rap on the door of the Clykes' dwelling. It did not come from the knocker, but sounded more like the blow from a great staff.

'Who on earth can that be at this hour?' said Longalio.

'Only one way to find out,' sniffed Calamorica, 'Sabrax,

get that will you.'

Sabrax got up from the table, all eyes in the room fixed on him as he went out from Long Hall into the hallway. He raised the latch and swung open the front door. Outside, beyond the step, in the moonlit evening, stood a glossy black raven.

'Raven? Is it you?'

The raven bowed.

'It is.'

'I hoped I might see you again one day to thank you. I know I failed to kill the hawk and I know it was you who got me safely down to earth. You kept your promise. My brother is safely home. Mother, mother, come quickly,' he shouted, 'all of you.'

The bird bowed again. The rest of the Clykes spilled out of the doorway. Gasps and loud whispers greeted the raven's presence. The bird bowed to them all.

'I know you won't believe it, but this is the bird,' said Sabrax excitedly, patting the raven, 'the one who helped me train and prepare in my attempt to kill the hawk.'

'You've no idea who this is?' asked Calamorica.

'It's a raven,' replied Sabrax.

'This is no ordinary bird, it is as you yourself said, "a wise old bird". Sabrax, this is Cataporinganio Clyke.'

There was a flash of light. The Clykes shielded their eyes and when they looked again, there stood the old wizard.

'Hello my brave friend.'

'You can turn yourself into a raven?'

'Or into a salmon, or a deer.'

Calamorica held out her arms. Cataporinganio embraced her.

'Thank you for returning the talisman to us, and for helping Sabrax, Dorcan and myself, of course.'

'It was the least I could do - after being invited as honoured guest to such a splendid birthnight party.'

Cataporinganio raised his hands. The talk and laughter among the Clykes subsided.

'You have been living through strange times recently, as all of you have been only too aware. Ye-ss. Brought on by the unfortunate loss of your talisman, I believe. A disastrous event, the knowledge of which was so skilfully kept from me.'

Cataporinganio stared at Calamorica, who gazed up nonchalantly at the night sky.

'And now it has been recovered. You have all been witness to a malevolent power at work, but you now know what can be achieved when it is resisted. I have had the honour of helping Sabrax, this brave, unselfish Clyke. He was willing to sacrifice his life for you all. I cannot think of any greater gesture of love and affection than that.'

The Clykes applauded and whistled.

'I think Sabrax is the one who should take on the role of keeper of the brooch,' said Calamorica, 'and we must make it official, here and now.' She gave her statement emphasis with a broad sweep of her arms.

Clykes looked at each other, wondering what was going to happen next. Cataporinganio strode into the wall, followed hastily by the rest of the Clykes. He stood in the centre of Long Hall. Calamorica went straight to the chimney breast, pushed the stone on the pivot and got the casket from its hiding place in the void. She pulled off her bonnet and handed both to Cataporinganio, who solemnly took them from her. Taking the brooch from its box, he deftly pinned it to the bonnet, while speaking in a tongue no one there understood. He raised the bonnet above his head and showed it to the Clykes.

'Please,' said Cataporinganio, gesturing with his hand to Sabrax, 'come forward.'

Sabrax stood up and walked to the centre of the room.

'Kneel down, please,' requested Cataporinganio.

'No,' he said, raising his hand.

'Sabrax? I think you should.'

'Let me speak - please.'

Loud muttering rose up from the Clykes, and they gave each other worried glances.

'Very well. Go on. Speak.'

Sabrax turned to face those in the room.

'We thought the loss of our brooch was the worst thing that could ever befall us,' he said, moving among them, 'and it was, for a time. What its loss did for us, however, was to show how strong and resilient we all are. From our misfortune, we have all emerged with honour. I realise now that I have around me family who are brave beyond belief. We have all helped to bring our brooch home, each and every one of us. I mention in particular my brave brother who, in spite of his fears, came with me on a task fraught with danger. But there are two especially who should be honoured, for without their determination and courage, we would still be suffering. If you are all agreed, I would like the brooch to be presented to Rosmanda and Woadica, to be held in their safe keeping. They saved my life, and in doing so released my mother and Dorcan from where they were trapped, within the hawk's thrall.'

156

Cataporinganio looked to Calamorica. She nodded her assent. And then to the rest of the Clykes, who nodded as one. All was sealed. Cataporinganio walked to where Rosmanda and Woadica stood. He raised the bonnet above Rosmanda's head.

'With all the powers I have in me and with the blessings of our ancestors,' he said, 'I proclaim you, Rosmanda and you, Woadica, keepers of the brooch.'

He placed the bonnet on Rosmanda's head. She smiled, reflected candlelight flashing from the facets within the jewel. Rosmanda took the bonnet from her head and handed it to Woadica, who put it on. Woadica grinned and patted it with her hand. Then she took off the bonnet. She unpinned the jewel and handed the bonnet to Calamorica. Woadica put the jewel back in its box and snapped the lid shut.

'Return the box to the safety of the wall, mother,' implored Woadica, handing it to her, 'and leave it there.'

'Far too precious to be worn,' held Rosmanda.

Calamorica walked across to the chimney breast, placed the box in the void and closed the stone over.

*

One week later, Cataporinganio had returned to his granite mountain. The window of his study was open and birdsong filled the evening air. He sat in his armchair in front of a glowing peat fire, warming his bare feet, smiling contentedly and drinking from a large goblet filled with fine wine. A tall earthenware jug containing more wine stood on the side table. His gaze travelled from the fire, over the white limestone mantelpiece, on up the wide chimney breast, to settle on the huge oak shield that now supported the stuffed and mounted head of his old adversary, Krokr Longtoe.

'And here you are at last. It was a long hard struggle to end your reign. But the right Clykes came along at the right time to stop you. Sabrax, the one you seized from the wall top, he does not know you killed his father. I will tell him one day.'

He raised up his goblet.

'I drink to the health of all Clykes and wish nothing but harm to those who would seek to injure them.'

He sank his wine and smiled.

'I sincerely hope that evil in the dale has died with you, Krokr Longtoe, but we shall see. We shall see.'

Glossary

mill race   channel carrying water to the mill
                         wheel

brose   drink made from oatmeal and
                         butter

purlins   timber roof beams

hawk waiting until   locking reflex in hawk's foot to
its talons fell open   ensure prey does not escape

fettle   make or repair

dry-stone walls   stone walls made without mortar

throughstones   tie the two faces of the stone wall
                         together

heartings   small broken stones used to fill the
                         interior of the walls

camstones   large top stones laid on wall to
                         discourage sheep from jumping
                         over

hogg hole   rectangular hole formed in drystone
                         wall for sheep to pass from field to
                         field

brandlings   small, red, wiry worms found in
                          leaf mould

stirrup and trigger   terms used to describe parts of a
                          crossbow

coins and rags at   the ancient custom of well dressing
the well